Frazer looked at his mother. 'I thought this work of yours was supposed to be a deadly secret. Bilbo and I haven't spoken to each other for three months because of i*, and now you're going to start scattering whales all over the place. You might as well put an ad in the pa: and charge folk four ecu to see Rye's Apparatus in .'

'N arling, don't exaggerate,' chided Harper. 'The oc a big place. When the whales are spotted, pe ill assume they've been hiding, that's all.'

'A sure, Mum? Won't it seem a bit strange, all the tinct species suddenly reappearing in pairs as th Noah's opened up his flipping Ark somewhere an all the animals out?'

Harper laughed out loud and clapped her hands. 'What a wonderful image, darling. Noah's Ark. It'd never struck me, but that's exactly what Rye's Apparatus *is*, isn't — a hi-tech Noah's Ark?' She shook her head. 'No, here's no danger. Even if someone does notice, a time machine's the *last* explanation they'll think of . . .'

Other titles available by Robert Swindells,
and published by Corgi Yearling Books

ABOMINATION

HYDRA

INSIDE THE WORM

JACQUELINE HYDE

NIGHTMARE STAIRS

ROOM 13

Also available, published by Doubleday Books

INVISIBLE!

TIMESNATCH

ROBERT SWINDELLS

Illustrated by Jon Riley

CORGI YEARLING

TIMESNATCH
A CORGI YEARLING BOOK : 0 440 86322 8

First published in Great Britain by Doubleday,
a division of Transworld Publishers Ltd

PRINTING HISTORY
Doubleday edition published 1994
Corgi Yearling edition published 1995

5 7 9 10 8 6

Set by Phoenix Typesetters

Corgi Yearling Books are published by Transworld Publishers,
61–63 Uxbridge Road, London W5 5SA,
a division of The Random House Group Ltd,
in Australia by Random House Australia (Pty) Ltd,
20 Alfred Street, Milsons Point, Sydney, NSW 2061, Australia,
in New Zealand by Random House New Zealand Ltd,
18 Poland Road, Glenfield, Auckland 10, New Zealand
and in South Africa by Random House (Pty) Ltd,
Endulini, 5a Jubilee Road, Parktown 2193, South Africa.

Printed and bound in Great Britain by
Cox & Wyman Ltd, Reading, Berkshire.

For Gabrielle

ONE

Butterflies don't know much. This one didn't know it was a chequered skipper – one of only sixty left in the world. It didn't know that this sun-dappled clearing was part of Rockingham Forest, and it certainly didn't know that its quick, darting flight was closely observed by three humans, two of whom weren't even born yet.

Heavy with the eggs it bore, the insect alighted on a leaf. At once the surrounding air became suffused with a soft, pulsating glow. The leaf trembled for an instant ever so faintly and when it stopped, the butterfly had gone.

'There you go, folks.' Harper Rye held up the flask for her children to see. 'One chequered skipper, extinct for twenty years yet very much alive, undamaged and beautifully pregnant. We've finally cracked it, my darlings.'

'Oh, Mum!' Kizzy, a ten-year-old version of her mother with the same straight dark hair and glasses, flung her arms round Harper's neck and kissed her on the mouth. 'I knew you'd do it. I *always* knew.'

'Steady!' Harper set down the flask before returning the child's embrace. 'Of course you did, my precious. Your faith in your old mum has been positively unswerving.'

'I knew you'd do it too,' growled Frazer. At thirteen he was less demonstrative than his sister and more cynical. 'What I *didn't* know was that you'd get all excited over butterflies and stuff when you could be snatching people. I mean, why can't we bring *Granny* back or something?'

Harper's grin faded as she looked at her son. 'Because, my love, the ability to create new technology carries with it heavy responsibilities. If we were to misuse my invention it might cause untold harm. For example, to snatch a human being – any human being – could alter history in some dramatic way we haven't even dreamed of. No.' She shook her head. 'Rule one *must* be – no humans.'

Frazer raked a hand through his mop of ginger curls. 'Hmmm. Never thought of that, Mum. Altering history, I mean. So that's why we're sticking to animals and plants – because that won't change history?'

'It *will*,' smiled Harper, 'but hopefully not in ways which will be harmful, or even particularly noticeable.'

Kizzy gazed at her mother's machine – a machine which could vanish and reappear like something in a magic show. It reminded her of an enormous doughnut. In fact, she'd christened it 'the Doughnut' without telling the other two. 'It's absolutely fantastic, Mum,' she breathed. 'What will you call it?'

'Oh – Rye's Apparatus, I expect. It's got a sort of ring to it, don't you think?'

Kizzy nodded. Better than the Doughnut, she thought.

'Rye's Apparatus.' Frazer rolled the words across his tongue a couple of times, then nodded. 'Ye-es. That sounds suitably historic, Ma – like Parkinson's Disease and Sod's Law. I reckon it'll do.'

Harper Rye laughed. 'I don't know about historic, my love. It might be best to keep this whole thing to ourselves, at least for the time being, but I know one thing – we'd better get this poor insect to Northamptonshire or it'll be forced to deposit its precious eggs in entirely the wrong place.'

TWO

It had begun four years earlier when physicist Harper Rye had noticed that certain subatomic particles were apparently capable of travelling back through time. At six, Kizzy had found the word 'physicist' too much to handle. As far as she was concerned, Mummy was a fizzy sister – a category which seemed to the child to describe her mother perfectly.

The initial discovery had given birth to an idea which had gripped Harper Rye, becoming almost an obsession. This in turn had triggered a successful application for funding to her old university, and a four-year bout of nonstop work which had driven her husband out of the family home in this isolated part of Suffolk and left the children very much to their own devices. For a couple of years they'd had a sort of nanny – a slow, amiable teenager named Pam who'd come from the village each morning to wash, dress and feed them, escort them to and from school and play with them, till she'd fallen in love and gone off to start a family of her own. They'd missed Pam terribly at first, but they'd learned to cope between them when Mum was busy, so that by the time Kizzy could say 'physicist' they were virtually independent.

Harper Rye's discovery had enabled her, after a tremendous amount of work, to design and construct a device which would travel back through time, snatch objects and convey them to her laboratory. The objects she intended to choose were plants and animals which once, not long ago, had inhabited the Earth but which had either been hunted or fished to extinction or wiped out by twentieth-century pesticides, urbanization or pollution. Her idea was to bring male and female specimens of such creatures into the cleaner, greener present, breed from them and release the offspring into the wild. In this way the consequences of past mistakes – of man's ecological vandalism – might be redeemed. Plants and animals which had vanished forever would reappear in 2039, enriching the earth once more with their variety.

And she'd done it, but not at first. At first, she'd encountered tremendous problems. There'd been problems of accuracy – of aiming her device at exactly the right spot at precisely the correct moment to capture a specimen. Then there'd been the problem of damage – precious specimens had arrived mangled or dead, or else in such a state of shock that they'd expired within a short time.

One by one the problems had been overcome, till now Harper Rye could guarantee to capture unharmed a creature as tiny, as fast-moving and as fragile as the chequered skipper which now rested inside its flask, the only chequered skipper in the world, as she drove the family car westwards along the A428 into Northamptonshire.

THREE

'Why d'you say we shouldn't tell anybody about your apparatus, Mum?' They'd released the butterfly and were cruising eastwards with the setting sun in the rearview mirror. The woman reached up and adjusted the glass till she lost the glare and found Frazer's puzzled face.

'You've read some history,' she said. 'Consider the fate of inventions. The aeroplane, for example. The first plane flew in nineteen hundred and three. The two guys who designed it probably thought they were giving the world a new, exciting sport or a fast, convenient means of getting from A to B. What they *didn't* foresee was that people would load bombs and guns on their machine and use it to slaughter one another, but that's exactly what they did.'

'Oh, yeah,' protested Frazer. 'But that was dead obvious, wasn't it? I mean, they should've known that would happen. I don't see how anybody could use Rye's Apparatus in a bad way.'

His mother smiled. '*You* don't see, darling, but believe me there are those out there who might.' She laughed briefly. 'You put an invention on the market – practically any invention – and somebody will find a way to use it as a weapon or to throw people out of work or to pollute the environment. When it comes to cruelty, greed and sheer stupidity, human ingenuity knows no bounds.'

Frazer pulled a face. 'Charming.'

'What'll happen to the butterfly?' asked Kizzy. The conversation was boring her. Her mother smiled. 'Well, my love, if we're lucky – *if* we're lucky – the butterfly will lay her eggs on a leaf. Hundreds of eggs. The eggs will hatch into hundreds of caterpillars, and some of those caterpillars – nine or ten perhaps – will survive to become butterflies next year. Those butterflies will mate and lay eggs and, before you know it, there'll be hundreds of chequered skippers in Rockingham Forest, just as there were a hundred years ago. But if we're *un*lucky,' she chuckled, 'a sparrow will eat our butterfly for breakfast first thing tomorrow morning.'

'Aw, Mu-um!'

'Well, darling, these things happen. We shan't know for ages, of course – a couple of years at least. Then, if no chequered skippers have been reported in the forest, we shall have to do the whole thing again.'

Frazer frowned. 'There's something I don't get.'

'*What* don't you get, dear?'

'The chequered skipper's extinct, right?'

'It *was*, yes.'

'Well – if it suddenly turns up again, won't people be curious? I mean, once a creature's extinct it's gone forever, isn't it?'

'Absolutely. But you see, darling, with something as tiny as the chequered skipper it's terribly hard to be certain. Nobody's *seen* one for twenty years, but when the species reappears they'll assume a few must've survived in a remote spot somewhere – that it wasn't extinct after all. That's why I chose to begin with something tiny.'

'Right.' Frazer grinned. 'It wouldn't work with a rhinoceros, would it?'

Harper shook her head. 'Not in Northamptonshire.'

They cruised on into dusk, laughing.

FOUR

The Ryes kept their secret for five months, during which time they re-established four species – two plants, a spider and an amphibian. It was while they were setting free their first birds that the trouble began.

It was a grey, blustery day in November. The Ryes had set off before dawn and had driven into Wales. At a remote location in the Brecon Beacons, Harper pulled over and switched off. It was almost midday but the road was deserted, the mountain landscape seemingly empty. The trio piled out of the Suzuki. Kizzy and

Frazer watched the road while their mother lifted out the basket. In the basket was a pair of red kites. Harper was unbuckling one of the straps which secured the lid when Kizzy hissed, 'Mum – look!' Harper glanced up. Two soldiers were approaching. 'Good Lord,' she murmured. 'Where on earth did *they* spring from?'

Kizzy shrugged. 'Out of the ground, it looked like.'

Her mother sighed. 'Never mind. Let me do the talking.'

'Morning.' The soldiers stepped on to the road. They weren't armed, but they didn't look particularly friendly. 'May I ask what you're doing?' one of them said.

Harper straightened up.

'Picnicking. Why – are we in a restricted zone or something?'

Instead of answering, the soldier nodded towards the basket. 'What's in there?'

'Food,' lied the physicist. 'Sandwiches and so forth. Why are you questioning us?'

'That's a livestock basket,' said the soldier. 'Odd thing to carry a picnic in. Open it, please.'

'Not till you tell me what this is about.'

'Madam, I must insist on your opening that basket.'

'And if I refuse?'

The soldier smiled fleetingly. 'Then *we'll* open it.'

Harper gazed at the man, who wore a captain's pips. 'What would you say, Captain, if I were to tell you that you were about to uncover a secret – a potentially dangerous secret?'

The captain smiled coldly. 'I'd say there is no such thing as a secret sandwich, nor a potentially dangerous sausage roll. Open the basket, please.'

'Oh, very well.' Harper squatted, undid the straps and raised the lid. A large bird rose in a clapping of wings to perch on the basket's rim. A loose feather whirled away on the wind. The captain gazed at the bird, then at the woman. 'Where did you get these creatures?'

Harper shook her head. 'I'm sorry, Captain – I can't tell you that.'

'Do you know what they *are*?'

'Yes. They're red kites.' As she spoke, the bird on the basket spread its wings, launched itself screeching into the air and wheeled away, followed at once by its mate. The second soldier side-stepped in a reflexive way with his arms spread, then, realizing the futility of his gesture, dropped his arms and stood watching the birds skim away, dwindling into the distance across a hillside. The captain said, 'The red kite was thought to be extinct. I must ask you once again how you came by these birds.'

'What *I* don't understand,' countered Harper, 'is what all this has to do with the Army. I mean – where did you spring from, and why are you so interested in birds, for goodness sake?'

'Most of this,' the captain indicated their surroundings with a sweep of his arm, 'is Ministry of Defence land. A lot of it is fenced off so people can't wander about, and it's become a sort of wildlife sanctuary.'

Harper chuckled. 'You're kidding, right?'

'No, I'm not.' The captain seemed nettled. 'Many rare species thrive on M.o.D. land. Some of them are found nowhere else, in fact, and we do what we can to protect them. That's why your basket worried us – it might have contained ferrets or falcons or something. We have to be careful, you see.'

'Good Lord.' The physicist shook her head. 'I must admit I've never thought of the Army as a guardian of the natural environment.' She looked at the captain. 'I think you'd better take me to your leader,' she said.

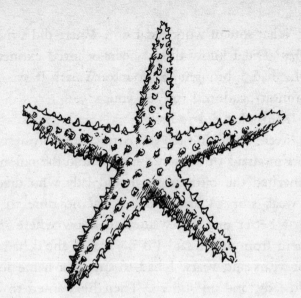

FIVE

'Where've you *been*, Mum?' demanded Kizzy as her mother climbed into the Suzuki. Frazer watched the army jeep do a three-point turn and speed away.

'I'm sorry, darlings.' The physicist fished for her keys. 'I'd no idea they'd keep me so long.'

'An hour and a half,' complained Kizzy. 'We thought you were never coming back.'

'What happened?' asked Frazer, as the jeep passed from sight.

'Oh.' His mother shrugged. 'They took me to see a colonel who asked me a lot of questions. Who was

I? What sort of work did I do? Where did I find the kites? Did I know they'd been believed extinct, and why had I brought them into Wales? It was quite an interrogation, I can tell you.'

'And what did you say?'

'Well, I couldn't tell the Army about my apparatus, so I'm afraid I invented a story. I told the colonel I'd inherited the birds from an old lady who died. It's a weak story, I know, but I had no time to think up a better one. He wanted to know where *she* got them from and I said I'd no idea – she'd had them for years and years. I had to invent a name for the old lady, and an address. Then he wanted to know what the secret was I'd mentioned to the captain. I said there *was* no secret – I'd just been hoping to make the captain leave us alone. Then he asked what I'd intended doing with the birds and I told him we meant to release them. I said the old lady had put it in her will that she wanted them released. He wrote everything down, but I don't think he believed me.'

'So what happens now?'

'I don't know, dear. I assume they'll check up, and when they find my old lady never existed they'll want to see me again.'

Frazer frowned. 'Doesn't that worry you, Mum?'

'Of course it does. The last thing I want is for the M.o.D. to come sniffing around, but if they do it can't

22

be helped. All we can do is carry on with the work, keep our eyes open for strangers and hope to be left alone.' She turned the key in the ignition and steered the Suzuki on to the narrow mountain road.

Kizzy looked back. 'I wonder what those kites are doing now,' she said.

SIX

A few days before the Christmas holidays Frazer said, 'Mum, can I have Bilbo to stay for a night or two during the hols?' They'd heard nothing more from the Army and were beginning to relax. Bilbo, whose real name was Andrew Baggins, had once been Frazer's best friend.

Harper sighed. 'I suppose you may,' she said, 'since you stayed with him last summer, but I thought the two of you had fallen out?'

Frazer nodded glumly. 'We have, but you know

what he's like. He's absolutely nuts on pond-life and creepy-crawlies in general, and because that's *your* field he's been badgering the life out of me to invite him to spend some time here.'

His mother nodded. 'And of course he can use your stay with him as a lever.' She sighed again. 'I'll spend the whole time fending off his questions about my work, and you'll wear yourself out keeping him away from the lab and from certain outbuildings.'

'It'll be all right, Mum, honestly. Bilbo's interested in the Roman foundations they uncovered near Earl Soham, so we'll be out with our bikes a lot of the time, and at night you can tell him all about your creepy-crawlies without mentioning Rye's Apparatus.'

And so it was arranged. Andrew would arrive on the twenty-eighth of December and stay till the fourth of January. Kizzy was not pleased.

'Ooh, yuk!' she cried. 'I can't stand Andrew Baggins. He's creepy.'

Creepy or not, Andrew arrived at the Ryes' sprawling farmhouse on the twenty-eighth in his father's Volvo. Frazer and his mother helped take in their guest's baggage while Kizzy sulked in her room. Baggins senior drank a cup of coffee, said goodbye to his son and set off back to Bury St Edmunds.

'So, Mrs Rye,' said Bilbo as they turned from waving his father off. 'What are you working on these days?'

Groaning inwardly, Harper forced a smile. 'Oh, nothing dramatic, I'm afraid. Still chasing those elusive particles of mine.'

'Really?' Bilbo beamed. 'I look forward to hearing all about it, Mrs Rye. I'm totally *nuts* on particles, you know.'

Bilbo had arrived in mid-afternoon, and by the time he'd unpacked and settled into his room it was dusk. Over dinner they talked about particles. Frazer kept yawning and Kizzy was so bored she wished she dare flick some of her peas at their guest with her knife crying, 'How d'you like *these* particles, creep?' But of course, she daren't. After dinner the two boys went off to Frazer's room to play video games while Harper and Kizzy cleared up.

''Tisn't fair,' grumbled Kizzy. 'I never have a friend to stay. All *I* get to do is clean up after *his* friends.'

'Now, Kizzy,' smiled Harper. 'It isn't like that and you know it. Tomorrow it'll be their turn to do the washing-up, and you can have a friend to stay at Easter. How's that?'

Kizzy shrugged. 'I'll still be glad when he's gone.'

Harper bent, tea-towel in hand, to whisper in her daughter's ear. 'So shall I,' she said.

SEVEN

Things went well for three days. The weather was dry and mild and the two boys spent most of the daylight hours biking. They visited Earl Soham to view the excavations and did the round of nearby villages. In other circumstances Kizzy would have accompanied her brother, but she had no wish to go biking with Andrew Baggins. After dusk, Bilbo showed no inclination to investigate the house or its grounds, being perfectly content with Frazer's games and CDs.

At teatime on the thirty-first, Harper Rye said, 'As it's New Year's Eve I thought we'd push the boat out

– have a bit of a party.' While the boys had been out, she and Kizzy had prepared a feast, Kizzy having been bribed into helping by the promise of a slap-up feed for herself and a friend at Easter.

The festivities went well and the quartet greeted the new year in style. It was twenty to one when Harper mentioned the time and the party finally broke up.

Next morning, everybody slept late except Bilbo, who woke at his usual time of six-thirty. He lay for a while listening for sounds of his hosts rising, but heard nothing. At seven he got up and went downstairs. There was nobody about.

Bilbo was now where he hated to be – at a loose end. There was some washing-up to be done from last night and he did this, certain that the noise he made would rouse the household, but when the last teaspoon stood gleaming in the drainer, all was silent. 'Well,' he told himself, 'I'm not wiping 'em as well. I'm off exploring.'

He let himself out through the kitchen door and found himself standing in a cobbled yard enclosed on three sides by outbuildings. It was still dark, but the light from the kitchen window was enough to see by and he began strolling around, hands in pockets, trying doors and peering through dusty windows. Most of the doors yielded readily enough, revealing the sorts of things he'd expected: stepladders, coiled hoses, garden tools, broken toys, discarded furniture. One or two were locked, and looking through the windows of these revealed nothing because of the dark inside. It was when he reached the last building – a low, lime-washed structure not far from the door he'd come out by – that he found something which made him catch his breath.

The building had only one small window. Peering through this, the boy saw a long fishtank standing on a bench. The tank had a hood from which light fell, illuminating the interior. By this light, Bilbo saw that the water in the tank was only a few centimetres deep above a layer of gravel. Here and there, large pebbles broke the surface, and on these pebbles lay a number of creatures which he recognized as newts. This would have been only moderately interesting, except that Bilbo was almost certain he was looking at specimens of the great crested newt, an amphibian which had died out forty years before.

EIGHT

'Frazer?'

'Uh-huh?' It was nine-thirty. The two friends were biking north towards Thetford.

'You know that white building in your yard?'

'Sure. What about it?' Frazer's response sounded cool but his heart kicked.

'I looked through the window. There's a fishtank.'

'That's right.'

'With newts in it.'

'So?'

'I – they looked like great cresteds to me.'

'Don't talk daft, Bilbo. The great crested's extinct. What you saw were smooths. They have crests, y'know, and orange bellies, just like cresteds had.'

Bilbo shook his head. 'They were big, Frazer – far too long for smooths. I reckon they're great cresteds.'

Frazer scoffed. 'They *can't* be, can they? The crested's extinct, old mate. It's gone. Maybe the glass magnified 'em, or you saw two lying together. After all, it must've been pretty dark at the time.'

'What d'you keep 'em for, Frazer?'

'Pets. They're Kizzy's.'

'Why's the door locked, then?'

'I dunno, do I? Ask Kizzy.'

'I want to see 'em, Frazer. Close up, when we get back.'

Frazer shrugged. 'That'll be up to Kizzy, Bilbo. You'll have gathered she's not exactly crazy about you.'

Bilbo nodded. 'I've gathered, but I'll ask her anyway. After all, it's not a lot to ask, is it?'

'Kizzy?' It was three-thirty, and dusk. In the porch the boys had shed their mud-spattered footwear and were wiping down their machines.

Kizzy scowled at Bilbo. 'What?'

'I saw your newts this morning.'

'My—' She intercepted her brother's warning

glance and forced a smile. 'Oh, yes. My newts. Cute little beauties, aren't they?'

'I'd like to take a look at them if you don't mind.'

'But you've seen them, Andrew. You said so.'

'Close up, Kizzy. I want to see them close up.'

'Oh, but I've – I've put them to bed. In the wild, they'd be hibernating at this time of year. I have to be very careful, especially at night. Keep them warm. I'll show you in the morning if you like.'

Bilbo propped his gleaming bike against the lime-washed wall and shook his head. '*Now*, Kizzy. Show me now – I've never seen a great crested before.'

Kizzy laughed. 'Great crested? You won't see one of *those* in my collection, you div. They're extinct.'

'Then show me, Kizzy. Fetch the key and show me. It's just across the yard.'

'Hello, boys!' Harper appeared in the doorway, smiling brightly. 'Good ride?' She looked at Bilbo. 'Show you what, Andrew?'

'Oh – newts, Mrs Rye. I'd like to see Kizzy's newts.'

'Oh, yes. The newts. Fascinating creatures. First thing tomorrow, Andrew, OK? Dinner's ready now.'

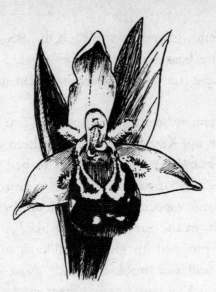

NINE

Bilbo's room looked out on the yard. He spent some time gazing across at the white building before getting into bed. Then he lay for a while wondering whether it was worth sneaking down in an hour or so and trying to find a key. He decided it wasn't. There was probably only one key, and Kizzy would have it in her room. Drowsing, he began a fantasy in which he crept into Kizzy's room and retrieved it, but he fell asleep before the bit where he'd open the outhouse door.

Harper Rye was not asleep. She spent some minutes

with Kizzy, then went to her room and read till all was quiet. Then she crept downstairs, slipped into a parka and left the house through the kitchen door.

At breakfast Bilbo gave Kizzy a sly look and said, 'This is it then, Kizzy – the day we see the newts.'

Kizzy caught her lower lip in her teeth and gazed at her plate. When she didn't reply the boy said, 'Well, Kizzy – are you ready?'

'There are no newts, Andrew,' she murmured. 'I let them go.'

Bilbo stared. 'You let them go? On the second of January?'

Kizzy nodded.

'But they'll die. You said yourself they'd normally be in hibernation. Why on earth did you do it, Kizzy?'

The girl shook her head. 'I dunno. They were mine. I guess I just didn't want anyone to see them.'

'Meaning me?'

'Meaning anyone, Andrew.'

'Where are they – when did you do this?' Bilbo had risen to his feet as if he meant to rush off and rescue the amphibians.

'Andrew.' Harper Rye spoke softly. 'Sit down, please.' Bilbo sat and the woman said, 'What Kizzy has told you is not quite true, and that's my fault.'

35

'Y-your fault, Mrs Rye?'

'Yes. *I* removed the newts. I asked Kizzy to tell you she released them. I realize now that I was wrong. You deserve the truth, which is that the creatures form part of an experiment I'm conducting. The work is at a very sensitive stage, and I'd very much prefer not to exhibit the newts for the time being. I can tell you they are safe and well, and I'm sure I can rely on you to pursue the matter no further.'

Bilbo's nod was dubious. 'I – I won't talk about it, Mrs Rye, honestly, but I have to ask. *Are* they great cresteds?'

The woman nodded. 'Yes, Andrew, they are, but you mustn't ask where I found them.'

Bilbo stared at his hands on the tablecloth for a while, then swallowed hard and looked up. 'The great crested is extinct,' he croaked. 'There's only one place you *could* have found them.'

TEN

'So where is it?' persisted Bilbo, as he and Frazer pedalled without haste beneath an over-arching vault of naked branches.

'Where's what?' There was irritation in Frazer's tone. He was all right, old Bilbo, but he never knew when to back off.

'Your mum's device, whatever it is. The thing she used to bring those newts back to life.'

'Back to life?' scoffed Frazer. 'Who d'you think Mum is – Frankenstein?'

Bilbo shook his head. 'Quit stalling, OK? There are

extinct creatures at your place. Your mum admitted it and I saw 'em with my own eyes. Something's going on – something big, and I think scientists should come clean about what they're doing. It's secret work that produces sinister developments.'

Frazer sighed. Bilbo was due to go home the day after tomorrow. He wished it could be today.

'Listen, Bilbo. There's no device for bringing things back to life, right? You have my word on that. Mum found some great cresteds somewhere and she's working with them, and that's all I can tell you.'

'Well, it's not enough, old pal.' Bilbo's tone was angry. 'It's like there's a conspiracy between the three of you to hide the truth. Next time there's a phone box I'm going to call Dad and have him come for me. I won't stay where I'm not wanted.'

'Hey, Bilbo – there's no need—'

Bilbo began to pedal furiously so that Frazer found himself shouting at his friend's receding back.

'There's no conspiracy, you div. Mum's work's a bit hush-hush, that's all. She's a scientist, for Pete's sake.'

It was no use. Bilbo found a phone box at Woolpit and, by the time Frazer caught up, he'd done it. Remounting he said, 'I'm off back, Frazer. Packing to do. Dad's coming at six.'

It was a miserable ride. Bilbo set a cracking pace

and it took Frazer all his time to keep up. They didn't speak. When they got home, Bilbo marched through the house without a word to anyone and went straight to his room.

'What's up with *him*?' asked Kizzy. She and Harper were playing Scrabble.

Frazer told them what had happened.

'Oh, dear.' Harper levered herself out of the armchair. 'How embarrassing. Perhaps if I go up—'

'No, Mum.' Frazer shook his head. 'Leave him. It's no use. I know him. Once he's got something fixed in his skull, nothing'll budge it. I just hope his dad doesn't think we've been trying to poison him or something.'

'Oh, Frazer.' His mother hugged him. 'I'm so sorry. I hate to see my work coming between you and your friends like this.'

''S OK.' Frazer broke away. 'My own fault anyway – I invited him.'

Kizzy gazed across at them. 'I suppose this is what it'll be like from now on,' she said. 'Everyone avoiding us, saying, "Odd lot, those Ryes. Secretive. Something fishy going on there if you ask me."' She giggled. 'Could be quite fun in a way.'

ELEVEN

January gave way to February and February slipped into March, and the Ryes heard nothing from the Army. They began to relax. Each weekday Harper drove her children to school in Bury St Edmunds and collected them at the end of the day, and the hours between were filled with work.

One evening in mid-March, when the washing-up was done and the family was sitting round the log-fire, Harper said, 'Newts and butterflies are easy, but what about whales?'

'What about 'em?' asked Frazer.

'What about Easter?' queried Kizzy. 'Can I have Jennifer to stay like you promised?'

Harper sighed. 'Yes, darling, you can have Jennifer to stay exactly as I promised.' She smiled. 'There's plenty of room for Jennifer, but a pair of sperm whales is another matter entirely.'

'I wasn't going to invite any sperm whales,' giggled Kizzy. 'Just Jennifer.'

'Shut up, Kizzy,' growled Frazer. 'What's this about whales, Mum?'

'Well.' Harper bent forward and thrust a log of applewood into the embers. 'Up to now, the creatures we've snatched from the past have all been small, which is just as well. I mean, it's easy enough to keep an orchid here, or a tankful of newts or a pair of kites, but what about larger creatures? What about whales?'

Frazer shrugged. 'Can't do anything about 'em, can we? There's no sea here, and we can hardly shove two sperm whales in the back of the Suzuki and drive 'em down to Felixstowe.'

Kizzy looked thoughtful. 'No, but do they need to come here in the first place?'

Harper smiled. 'Go on, darling.'

'Well, what if you could snatch 'em from the past and have the Dough— I mean, have Rye's Apparatus deliver 'em straight to the seaside?'

'Why not indeed,' nodded Harper.

41

'Because it's not possible,' said Frazer. 'The specimens end up where the apparatus reappears, surely?'

His mother shook her head. 'Not necessarily, darling. Not any more. I've been slaving away all winter, using starfish.' She smiled. 'Yesterday I snatched a starfish from twenty-five years ago and placed it in the sea off Dunwich and it didn't even notice it'd moved.'

The boy gaped. 'So now you're thinking of—'

'Exactly. I'm thinking of locating some sperm whales, snatching a pair and slipping them into the ocean somewhere. I *think* our oceans have cleansed themselves of the muck our ancestors poured into them. Plankton populations are certainly up. I need to see whether whales can live in them once more.'

'But they'd be noticed, surely – things that size?'

Harper nodded. 'They'd be spotted eventually, no doubt. But so what?'

'So what?' Frazer looked at his mother. 'I thought this work of yours was supposed to be a deadly secret. Bilbo and I haven't spoken to each other for three months because of it, and now you're going to start scattering whales all over the place. You might as well put an ad in the paper and charge folk four ecu to see Rye's Apparatus in action.'

'Now, darling, don't exaggerate,' chided Harper. 'The ocean's a big place. When the whales are spotted, people will assume they've been hiding, that's all.'

42

'Are you sure, Mum? Won't it seem a bit strange, all these extinct species suddenly reappearing in pairs as though Noah's opened up his flipping Ark somewhere and let all the animals out?'

Harper laughed out loud and clapped her hands. 'What a wonderful image, darling. Noah's Ark. It'd never struck me, but that's exactly what Rye's Apparatus *is*, isn't it – a hi-tech Noah's Ark?' She shook her head. 'No, there's no danger. Even if someone *does* notice, a time machine's the *last* explanation they'll think of.' She grinned. 'I've decided there's such a thing as being *too* cautious.'

Frazer shrugged. 'Maybe you're right, Mum. I certainly hope so.' He chuckled. 'It only needs one Bilbo-type character to start putting two and two together and our secret's blown wide open.'

TWELVE

On April 3rd 2040, the following brief item appeared in the *Bury St Edmunds Gazette*:

> *Great crested newts, believed by scientists to have died out many years ago, have been found living in a pond near the village of Lenton. The discovery, made by children, is causing ripples in the scientific community, and the pond, known locally as Froglet Pond, has been designated a site of special scientific interest.*

THIRTEEN

On the first day of the Easter holidays, while Kizzy entertained Jennifer and Frazer kept out of the way, Andrew Baggins went to his local library. He pressed the buzzer on the information desk and, when the assistant appeared, he handed her a newspaper clipping.

'This was in Wednesday's *Gazette*,' he said. 'Can you tell me how to find out whether anything else like that has been printed in other papers?'

The assistant read the item. 'You mean, about great crested newts?'

Bilbo shook his head. 'No – about anything. Any

creature that was supposed to be extinct being seen alive.'

'Well—' The woman frowned. 'There's a computer service that searches for items under various headings, but whether it'll have anything about extinct creatures, I don't know. I could try it for you, but there's a charge and it might take a while.'

Bilbo nodded. 'That's OK. Shall I come back tomorrow?'

The assistant smiled. 'Better make it the day after. If there *is* anything, I'll have printouts ready for you then.'

'Fine,' said Bilbo. He hummed 'Comin' Through the Rye' and smiled grimly to himself as he left the library.

FOURTEEN

'Mrs Rye?' The man on the step was short and wore a grey suit.

'*Doctor* Rye,' corrected Harper. 'How may I help you?'

The man fished in an inside pocket and flashed an ID card. 'Morton's my name, Doctor Rye. I'm with the Ministry of Defence. You released a pair of red kites in the Brecon Beacons last November, is that correct?'

'Yes.'

'And you claimed to have inherited the birds from

a Miss Olivia Wentworth of – let me see.' He unfolded a small square of paper. 'Of Waterside House,
Walsham-le-Willows.'

'That is correct.'

'Well, no, Doctor Rye, that is *not* correct. There
is no Waterside House at Walsham-le-Willows, and
nobody seems to have heard of Miss Wentworth.'

'Oh,' murmured Harper.

Morton nodded. 'We thought perhaps you'd care
to try again.'

'Try again?'

'Another story. The truth, perhaps.'

'The truth?' Harper smiled fleetingly. 'Very well,
Mr Morton, you shall have it. The truth is that I have
a time machine.'

Morton gazed at her coldly. 'This isn't a game,
Doctor Rye. I'm here as a government representative
with powers you probably wouldn't believe. If you
persist in lying to me, you might well find yourself
in a great deal of trouble. I'm going to give you one
more chance to tell me the truth.'

Harper sighed. 'I've *told* you the truth, Mr Morton.
I've got a time machine. It's in the house. If you'll
follow me, I'll show it to you.'

'Rubbish!' snapped Morton. 'D'you think I'm an
utter fool?' He gave Harper no time to answer but
went on, 'Very well, if that's the way you want it

I'll bid you good-day, but I can assure you that you haven't heard the last of this – not by a long chalk.'

Harper watched from the step as the man spun on his heel and strode towards his chauffeur-driven car. 'Oh, dear,' she sighed.

FIFTEEN

Bilbo gazed at the printout. 'Four – the computer found four?'

The assistant nodded. 'One's the item from the *Gazette* – the one you showed me – but there are three others.'

'Great!' The boy's eyes gleamed behind the round lenses of his spectacles. 'How much do I owe you?'

'That'll be just two ecu, please.'

Bilbo paid, carried the printout to one of the study tables, and sat down. The first item was from something called the *Kettering Times*. It said:

Mr Trevor Sanderson of Market Harborough has caused a flutter among lepidopterists with his claim to have spotted a chequered skipper butterfly on a railway embankment near Bugbrooke. A spokesperson for the Northamptonshire Lepidoptery Association told our reporter, 'Mr Sanderson is almost certainly mistaken. The chequered skipper became extinct about twenty years ago.' In our picture, Mr Sanderson is pointing to the spot where he claims he saw the butterfly.

'Hmmm.' Bilbo moved on to the next piece, a three-liner from the *Merthyr Tydfil Advertiser*:

Police have arrested a man for allegedly shooting dead a red kite on M.o.D. land near Glyntawe. The red kite was thought to be extinct.

The last item had appeared in the *Princes Risborough Bugle*. It read:

Conservationists have mounted a round-the-clock vigil over a rare orchid found growing at an undisclosed location in the Chilterns. A spokesman would give no details, but said the orchid was of a type believed to have died out many years ago.

'So.' Bilbo sat back, took off his spectacles and

began polishing a lens with his handkerchief. 'Four examples. Three creatures and a plant, all thought to be extinct, all reappearing the same year. Coincidence?' He chuckled, replacing his glasses. 'No chance.'

He stood up, folded the printout and went back to the desk.

'Excuse me?' he said to the woman.

'Yes?'

'Could you find me the phone number of the *Sunday Sportsman?*'

The woman nodded. 'I think so.' She slid a fat volume towards her and flicked through it. 'Yes, here it is.' She read out the number. Bilbo wrote it on the back of the printout.

'Thanks.'

'You can phone from here, you know – there's a pay-phone in the foyer.'

Bilbo shook his head. 'I won't be phoning them just yet,' he smirked. 'I'm not quite ready.'

SIXTEEN

Jennifer Stone hated boys. They were loud and messy and rude. She was glad she and Kizzy had got through the holidays without Frazer wanting to tag along. So when she saw Andrew Baggins loitering as she took a shortcut through the churchyard on the day school started again, she groaned to herself. Andrew was the sort of boy who picked up worms and messed about with creepy-crawlies. You never knew what boys like Andrew might be hiding in their pockets.

'Hi, Jenny.' Bilbo's pale eyes weren't smiling. 'How was your stay with the Ryes?'

'It was good. Kizzy and I had a great time.' Why do you want to know? she wondered. And why are you blocking my way?

'See the newts, did you?'

'Newts?' Jennifer shivered. Is that what he's got in his pocket? 'No, I didn't, and I wouldn't want to.'

'Why not? Interesting creatures, newts. *I* saw 'em.'

'Good. Can I come past, please – it's ten to nine?'

Bilbo shook his head. 'Not yet. I want to ask you something first.'

'Well, hurry up then.' She wished someone would come by – a teacher perhaps – but nobody did.

'How long were you at their place?'

'Four nights.'

'Did you see or hear anything unusual at all?'

Jennifer shook her head. 'I don't think so.'

'You sure?' Bilbo's hand went to his jacket pocket. 'Seen a mole, have you? Close up? Dead?'

'Ugh!' Jennifer took a step backwards. 'No, I haven't. I'd be sick.'

'I've got one here, Jenny. It's gone stiff and it pongs a bit, but its coat's like velvet. It'd feel lovely sliding down the back of your neck. Are you absolutely certain nothing happened at Kizzy's?'

'Well—' Jennifer's eyes were on the boy's pocket.

'There *was* one thing. It was nothing, really. Just something Kizzy said when we were lying in the grass. She talks to herself sometimes.'

Bilbo came a step closer. His hand was in his pocket. Jennifer fancied she could smell the mole. 'What did she say, Jenny?'

'She said, "I wonder what our chequered skipper's doing at this moment?" I know it sounds stupid, but I thought she meant her dad. Her dad left, you know. I thought maybe he'd been a sailor or something and "our chequered skipper" was their pet name for him.'

Bilbo chuckled briefly. 'So what did *you* say?'

'I said, "pardon" or something like that, and she said, "nothing", sort of sharply, as if I was prying.'

'Then what?'

'Then she sat up and looked down at me and said, "Forget what I said just now, Jenny. If you're my friend, forget it." I didn't know what she was on about. I still don't.'

Bilbo smiled. 'Excellent. Do you know what a chequered skipper *really* is, Jenny?'

The girl nodded. 'It's a butterfly. I looked it up.'

'Right.' Bilbo removed his hand from his pocket. 'If you're my friend, Jennifer – mine and my mole's –

not a word to anyone about our little talk this morning. OK?'

Jennifer gulped and nodded. 'OK.'

'Fine.' Bilbo grinned and stepped aside. 'Off you go then – don't want to be late, do we, first morning back?'

SEVENTEEN

'Know what my dad reckons?' It was breaktime. Boys lolled about the bike sheds. Some smoked. Others, glassy-eyed and jiggling, were wired for sound. A few talked. Frazer looked at Stanton Sefton, who liked to be called SS.

'What does your dad reckon?' Frazer disliked Sefton and never called him SS. He didn't give a damn what the moron's dad reckoned, but talking passed the time.

'He reckons what this country needs is Hitler.'

'Oh, does he?' Frazer faked interest. 'He's the guy started World War Two, right?'

The other boy nodded.

'And gassed millions of people.'

'Yep.'

'So how come this country needs a guy like that?'

'Discipline, my dad says. Keep folk in line.'

Frazer nodded. 'Do what I say or be bumped off, you mean?'

'Right.'

'Sounds terrific. And I bet your dad'd volunteer to be commandant of one of the camps, wouldn't he – a death camp?'

Sefton nodded. 'That's exactly what he says. Here – how'd you know that, Rye?'

Frazer smiled. 'A guess, Sefton. A lucky guess.' He nodded and moved away, but for some reason he couldn't get Sefton's words out of his head.

EIGHTEEN

'Hello?' Andrew Baggins watched the teatime traffic through the clear plastic hood of the telephone kiosk. 'Is that the *Sunday Sportsman*?'

'Ye-es. How may I help you?'

'I'd like to speak to Harvey Parvin, please.'

'Is Mr Parvin expecting your call?'

'Not unless he's telepathic, but he'll want to hear what I have to tell him.'

'Yes, well – if you'll give me your name, I'll see if he's in.'

'Baggins. Andrew Baggins.'

'And how old are you, Mr Baggins?'

Bilbo sighed. 'Fifteen. How old are *you*?'

'Hold the line, please.'

There was a burst of rousing orchestral music, followed by a grunt. 'Parvin.'

'Oh, hi, Mr Parvin. My name's Baggins. Friends call me Bilbo. I've got a lead for you.'

'Is that right?' The journalist sounded less than thrilled. 'Go on then – what is it?'

'Do you – er – d'you pay for information, Mr Parvin?'

'Sometimes. Depends. Tell me what you've got.'

Bilbo hesitated. 'It's going to sound daft over the phone, Mr Parvin. Can't we meet? I've documents to show you.'

'Look, Mr Baggins, I'm a busy man. I can't just drop what I'm doing and rush out to meet some kid who says he's got a lead. You're going to have to *interest* me, son. Know what I mean?'

'Yes. Would a time machine interest you at all?'

There was a brief silence. It had begun to drizzle. Droplets beaded the hood, distorting Bilbo's view.

'Now listen, son. I told you I was busy. I don't have time for silly games. The *Sunday Sportsman*'s a newspaper, not a sci-fi mag, so if you don't mind I'm going to hang up now and get on with—'

'No!' cried Bilbo. 'Don't hang up. Listen, please.'

Speaking rapidly, he told the journalist what he'd seen at the Ryes' place, and about his discoveries since. When he'd finished there was another silence, broken only by the swish of tyres on wet tarmac. Then Parvin said, 'OK, son, it's just possible you've stumbled on something, though it sounds pretty far-fetched to me. D'you know the Hammer and Anvil at Long Melford?'

'The pub?'

'That's right. I'll meet you there at two o'clock tomorrow, OK?'

'I'll have to wag off school.'

The journalist chuckled. 'Even better then, isn't it?' He hung up.

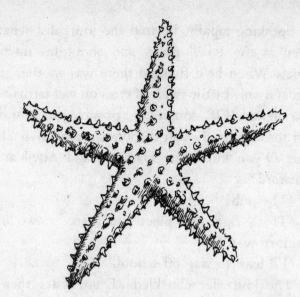

NINETEEN

When farmer Stan Rickerby glanced out of the kitchen window that Tuesday morning, he expected to see what he always saw – forty Friesian cows dotted across the nine-acre meadow, chewing the cud and waiting to be milked. In fact, he was so certain he'd see this that he glanced and looked away, then uttered an exclamation and looked again.

The cows stood in a corner by the hedge, gazing at an enormous grey mound which occupied the middle of the field. For a moment, Stan thought someone must have come in the night and dumped ten truckloads of rubbish, but then the mound moved and his jaw dropped. 'It's— It looks like—' He knuckled his eyes, looked again and staggered to the phone.

'Hello – is that Janet?' Janet was married to the local bobby. 'Stan here, Janet. Stan Rickerby. Is John there? Yes, please.'

He stood jiggling the phone till the constable said, 'John here – what's the problem, Stan?'

'There's – I've just looked out and there's a whale in the nine acre.'

'A *what*?'

'A whale – or maybe it's a whacking gurt fish, I dunno.'

'Have you been at the scrumpy, Stan?'

'No, I haven't. It's there all right, whatever it is, and I want you to come out and take a look.'

'Have *you* had a look, Stan – a close one, I mean? How big's this thing?'

'I dunno, John. I only seen it through the window, but it's big – like three, four buses, I reckon. And it moved.'

The policeman sighed. 'OK, Stan, I'll be with you in ten minutes. Better stand clear till I get there.'

'Th-thanks, John.' The farmer's hand shook as he put down the phone. He muttered to himself and shook his head as he returned slowly to the window.

TWENTY

Breaktime round the bike sheds. Stanton Sefton laughs out loud, removing his headphones. 'Hey – anyone tuned local?'

Nobody is. Sefton laughs again. 'You'll never guess the latest newsflash.'

'Don't tell me,' growls Frazer. 'Hitler's been spotted at Orford, right?'

'Close, kid,' laughs Stanton. 'Try again.'

Frazer shakes his head. 'Can't be bothered, Stanton. Tell us.'

'They found a whale in the middle of a field at Westleton.'

A chorus of derision greets this announcement. Somebody snatches Sefton's 'phones and tries to listen in, while somebody else hacks at his shin with a trainer. Only Frazer is silent. He watches the developing mêlée for a moment, then turns and begins running towards the school building.

'Mum?'

'Frazer? Where are you? Is something wrong?'

'I'm calling from school, Mum. Nothing's wrong – at least, not here. Did you do the whale snatch last night?'

'Well, yes, darling, as a matter of fact I did, but I don't think we should be discussing it over the phone, and anyway how did you know?'

'You missed, Mum. Your whale's in a field at Westleton. It's on the news.'

TWENTY-ONE

'Yes, sir?' The landlord beamed at Bilbo across the bar of his almost empty lounge.

'Oh, I'm – I'm meeting somebody here. Two o'clock. Do you have Coke?'

'Certainly, sir. Ice and lemon?'

'Oh, yes please, that'll be great.'

'Take a seat and I'll bring it to you.'

Bilbo sat at a copper-top table with a green glass ashtray on it. The room's only other occupant – a very old man in a stained and shiny waistcoat – stared at him from a far corner. Bilbo avoided his gaze, pretending to study the sporting prints on the walls till his drink arrived.

'That'll be one fifteen, sir.'

'One—?'

Bilbo flushed, groping through his pockets, thinking, No wonder there's nobody here. He found the money, but it was a close thing.

'Thank you, sir.' The landlord waddled off. Bilbo sat gazing into the most expensive drink he'd ever bought. It was five to two.

'Mr Baggins?'

Bilbo, who'd been daydreaming, looked up with a start. 'Y-yes, that's me.'

'Harvey Parvin.' The man stuck out a hand. They shook briefly and Parvin sat down. He was a shortish, thickset man of about thirty-five with a dark, bushy moustache and a head of curly hair. He wore a black leather jacket and jeans. The landlord came over and the journalist ordered a pint of lager. He didn't speak till it had been delivered and he'd taken a long pull.

'So – what is it you've got to show me, son?'

Bilbo fished in an inside pocket. 'I know you think it's far-fetched,' he said, 'but—'

'No.' Parvin shook his head. 'No, I don't. Not any more. Not after what I've seen this morning. Show me.' Bilbo passed him the printout. Parvin unfolded it, smoothed it out and read rapidly, grunting and nodding at intervals. 'OK.' He gazed at Bilbo. 'I'd like to hang on to this. These people – the Ryes – I'll need their address.'

Bilbo gave it. Parvin wrote it down on a pad. Bilbo said, 'What *did* you see this morning?'

The journalist smiled. 'Only a whale, that's all. An extinct whale, alive, in the middle of a field two miles from the sea.'

Bilbo's eyes widened. 'Really? A whale? So what're you going to do next, Mr Parvin?'

Instead of answering the man said, 'Have you got a bank account, son?'

Bilbo shook his head. The journalist sighed, produced a fat wallet and counted out some notes which he folded and passed across the table. 'There you go – there's fifty E there. That's for the information you've given me, and for your discretion. Know what discretion means, do you?'

Bilbo shook his head and the man sighed again.

'Discretion means you don't tell anybody you've spoken to me, you don't give anybody else the information you've just sold to me – it's *mine* now – and you don't ask me what I'm going to do next. *That's* discretion.'

Bilbo nodded. 'I – I didn't do this just for the money, Mr Parvin. I wouldn't want you to think that. I did it because I believe scientists ought to—'

The man looked at him. 'I don't give a monkey's what you did it for, sunshine,' he growled. 'You've had my money, so as far as I'm concerned you're bought and paid for. Finish your drink, stand up and walk out. Don't say anything, don't look back, and don't come near this pub again till you're eighteen. Cheers.' He lifted his glass and drank deeply and, when he put it down, Bilbo had gone.

TWENTY-TWO

Harper Rye tuned into Heartbeat when her son rang off and stayed tuned all day. Every hour the station broadcast a news bulletin, and today each bulletin was an update on the whale story. Early updates just called it a whale, but later, as experts began arriving on the scene, it became a sperm whale, a female sperm whale, and a female sperm whale long thought to be extinct. Harper fretted, wondering how long it would be before the national media picked up the story.

She didn't know what to do. She wished she could snatch the whale again – make it vanish from the meadow at Westleton and drop it in the sea off Dunwich where its mate was presumably waiting, but Rye's Apparatus wasn't geared to snatch things from the present. She could only sit tight, listening to the updates, hoping somebody would come up with an explanation as to how the creature might have got where it was – an explanation which didn't involve a time machine, and which people would accept.

There were plenty of theories. One man thought there must have been a freak tidal wave during the night – a wave which swept four kilometres inland and left the creature stranded. Another said the whole thing would probably turn out to be a student prank or a publicity stunt to advertise washing powder. It was a sign from God, a mass hallucination and a message from outer space. From the depth of her distress, Harper found time to marvel at the number and variety of screwballs in our midst. It consoled her to learn that concerned, sensible people were at the scene too. The whale was still alive, and teams from Greenpeace and the Whale and Dolphin Conservation Society were involved in what was described as a race against time to devise a way of getting the creature into the sea.

At three o'clock it was time to go for Frazer and Kizzy. Harper walked out to the Suzuki. All seemed normal, which probably meant nobody linked the whale incident to her. It's only a matter of time though, she told herself gloomily, remembering Morton of the M.o.D. She climbed in and started the engine. As the Suzuki swung out of the driveway, its nearside door brushed the shrub behind which Harvey Parvin was crouching.

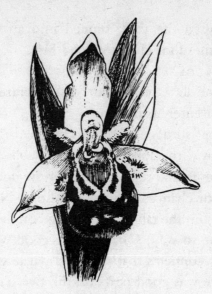

TWENTY-THREE

He worked his way round the outside of the house, trying doors and looking in windows. The doors were all locked and the windows he could see through revealed only the sorts of things you'd expect to find in a house. There was a wing whose windows were covered by pull-down blinds, which was frustrating. He considered breaking in, but decided to check the outbuildings first. Like Bilbo before him, he opened doors and peered through dark windows, but found nothing of interest. He was examining the lock on the kitchen door when he heard the Suzuki returning.

He crossed the yard, slipped into an outhouse and pulled the door closed behind him.

'So what do we *do*, Mum?' asked Frazer as the three of them entered the house.

Harper shrugged. 'I don't know, darling. We can't run away – the apparatus isn't portable. We *could* lock ourselves in and refuse to answer the door, but I don't fancy our chances against the M.o.D. No.' She threw the keys on the table and switched on the radio. 'We'll just have to wait. Carry on the good work and hope nobody connects that poor old whale with us.'

There was good news on the five o'clock bulletin. Using a low loader and keeping the whale wet with bedsheets and buckets of water, Greenpeace and the Whale and Dolphin Conservation Society had succeeded in getting the creature to the sea. It was in the sea now, off Dunwich. Heartbeat's reporter-on-the-spot could see it clearly from where she was standing. It didn't seem to be doing much, she told her listeners – lying on the surface two hundred metres beyond the surf, shaken perhaps by its ordeal but definitely alive.

'Well,' smiled Kizzy as Harper switched off. 'That's *something*, I suppose.'

Dinner was a subdued affair. When it was over Kizzy said, 'It's Frazer's turn to wash up, Mum. I'm off biking.'

Harper looked at her. 'Be careful, darling. Watch the traffic, don't talk to anyone and be home well before dark.'

'Aw, *Mum*!' sighed Kizzy. 'I *know*. I'm not a baby, for goodness sake.'

'You're *my* baby,' smiled Harper. 'You always will be, so you might as well get used to it.'

Kizzy crossed the yard to the outbuilding where she kept her bike. Harvey Parvin saw her coming and got down behind a mildewed sofa. He'd just had an idea and it was making him smile.

TWENTY-FOUR

Kizzy heard the car behind her and pulled over to the left. 'Come on then,' she murmured, accustomed to the impatience of drivers. 'Pass me – I'm not stopping you.' She was a mile from the village, in a place where the road passed through dense woodland. Trees overhung the lane on either side, shutting out the sun, forming a dim green tunnel which made Kizzy imagine she was cycling underwater.

The car was close behind now, going at a crawl, making no effort to overtake. Kizzy glanced back. It was a blue Mazda. The man behind the wheel seemed to be smiling. Some words of her mother's came into her head. Funny men. Never get in anybody's car, Harper had said. There are funny men about. Mum called them funny, but Kizzy knew that the sort of men she was talking about weren't funny at all. They were scary. They liked to hurt children, or even kill them. She put on a spurt, pedalling as fast as she could. The driver accelerated to stay close behind. Oh Lord, breathed Kizzy. What now? What shall I *do*?

Stop, said a voice in her head. If you stop he'll have to pass. She pulled over and stopped, propped on her left leg, listening, praying that the car would go by.

It didn't. It came scrunching up and stopped beside her. The nearside window was down. The driver leaned across, smiling. He had a moustache and curly hair. He reminded Kizzy of someone she'd seen on the telly. 'Hello,' he said. His eyes twinkled. 'You're Kizzy, aren't you?'

Kizzy was startled. How did he know her name? She was sure she'd never seen him before. Instead of replying she set off again, standing on the pedals, wobbling. The car rolled forward, staying level. Kizzy stopped. The car stopped too. The driver was laughing. 'Don't keep running away,' he said. 'I only want to talk to you.'

'What about?' Kizzy was tense. If he opens his door I'm off, she thought.

'Get in the car.'

'Get lost — d'you think I'm stupid or something? My mum's told me about men like you.'

The man chuckled. 'Funny men, you mean?'

Kizzy flushed. 'How did *you* know?'

'Your mum's right, sweetheart. They're everywhere, but I'm not one of them. I chase information, not little girls. I think you've got some information for me, Kizzy.'

Kizzy shook her head. 'I don't think so.'

'Oh yes you have, sweetheart. I know you have. A little bird told me.'

'What bird?'

'The lesser-spotted Bilbo bird. You know the Bilbo bird, don't you?'

Kizzy nodded. 'So *that's* how you knew my name. Yes, I know Bilbo. He's a creepazoid, like you.'

'Now, now!' The man wagged a stubby finger, jokily severe. 'There's no need to be abusive, young woman. Tell me about your mum's machine.'

'Machine?' Kizzy frowned. 'I don't know what you mean. Mum hasn't got a machine, unless you mean the washing machine.'

He shook his head. 'I don't mean the washing machine, Kizzy. I mean the newt machine. The red kite machine. The whale machine.' He leaned closer. He wasn't smiling now. 'What I'm talking about is the *time* machine, sweetheart. Tell me about that.'

'No.' Kizzy shook her head. 'I don't know what you mean. I have to go home now.'

'You'll go home,' purred the man, 'just as soon as you give me the information.'

'And if I don't – what then?'

'Ah, well – then I just might have to turn into one of those funny men your mum warned you about.'

Fear washed over Kizzy, making her tremble. This was a lonely spot. Nobody had passed by while they'd been speaking. All the man had to do was bundle her into the car and drive off and nobody would ever see her again. They'd find her bike on the verge. Nothing else. She was helpless.

'All right,' she murmured. 'Promise you'll let me go and I'll tell you.'

'Now that's *much* better, sweetheart.' The smile was back. 'I'm right, aren't I – there *is* a machine?'

'Well—' As Kizzy opened her mouth, a girl of about her own age appeared round a bend and came pedalling towards them. Kizzy gasped with relief as she recognized Gabrielle Kromer, a classmate who lived in the neighbouring village of Elmswell.

'Gabrielle!' She called and waved. The other girl waved back and began to slow down. The man muttered something very rude and revved his engine. As Gabrielle steered her bike towards Kizzy, the Mazda shot forward in a cloud of blue exhaust and roared off round the bend.

'Who was that?' Gabrielle pulled up and gazed after the car.

'Oh, nobody,' smiled Kizzy. 'Just some guy wanting information.'

'Oh.' Gabrielle nodded. 'A tourist.'

'Something like that,' said Kizzy.

TWENTY-FIVE

'A man?' Harper's eyes widened. 'What man, darling – what did he want?'

Kizzy peeled off her jacket. 'I didn't know him, Mum. He was old – older than you, with a moustache and curly hair. He wanted information about the apparatus.'

'Did he *call* it that – the apparatus?'

'No, he called it a machine. Your mum's machine, he said.'

'But how did he know *you*, darling?'

Kizzy pulled a face. 'He'd talked to Andrew Baggins.'

'Bilbo? But what could Bilbo have told him, Kizzy?'

Kizzy shrugged. 'I dunno, Mum. The guy mentioned newts and red kites and whales. I don't see how Baggins could know about any of that, but he must've told him about me and given this address.'

Frazer walked into the room. 'What's the dreaded Bilbo been up to now?' he asked. Kizzy told him.

'Well, the rotten little plonker! You wait till I get my hands on him tomorrow.'

Harper shook her head. 'That's not going to help, Frazer. The damage is already done.'

'I bet he got money,' growled Frazer. 'He'd kill for money, that Bilbo. He's always been a miser.'

Harper looked at Kizzy. 'What did you tell the man, darling?'

'Nothing. I was going to, though – he scared me – but then Gabrielle showed up and he drove off.'

'Gabrielle?'

'Gabrielle Kromer from school.'

'Well, thank goodness for Gabrielle, that's all I can say.' Harper gave her daughter a hug. 'I'm afraid you'll have to stop biking off by yourself, darling – my nerves won't stand it.'

'Aw, Mu-um.'

'So who d'you reckon this guy was?' asked Frazer.

His mother shrugged. 'I don't know. Could be M.o.D. Could be the Press. Could be anybody. If I had to guess, I'd say he's a journalist on one of the tabloids. They'll stoop to anything to get what they want. We'll probably be headline news tomorrow.'

'But Kizzy didn't tell him anything,' cried Frazer.

Harper shook her head. 'From what he told Kizzy, it seems he's got half the story already. If he's like most of his colleagues he'll invent the rest.'

'So what do we *do*?'

Harper smiled grimly. 'We beat him to it, my darlings. Spoil his nice little exclusive.'

Kizzy frowned. 'How, Mum?'

'Simple. We contact the Press. Tell 'em everything.'

Frazer gazed at her. 'And then?'

His mother shook her head. 'Who knows?' she said.

TWENTY-SIX

It was awful. More awful than any of them had dreamed it could be. Harper Rye faxed her hastily drafted press release to the national dailies at nine o'clock that Tuesday evening, and by half-past ten their home was under siege. The driveway became totally blocked with vehicles out of which poured reporters, photographers and TV crews, clogging the yard and garden, lugging their paraphernalia from place to place as they jostled for positions near doors and windows. Luckily, the Ryes had locked up and drawn all the curtains before anybody arrived, but this didn't prevent people from pounding on doors, rapping at windows and shouting through the letterbox. At eleven-thirty, Harper, hoarse from shouting 'go away' and seething with anger, flung open an upstairs window and yelled, 'For God's sake stop this insane racket and get off my property – my kids have school tomorrow.'

She might as well have saved her breath. At the sound of her voice there was a frantic surge towards the open window. Cameras flashed. Microphones like fluffy toys on sticks swayed at sill-height and somebody bellowed, 'Talk to us, Doctor Rye – the public has the right to know the truth.'

'Truth?' croaked Harper. 'Half of you wouldn't recognize the truth if it came up and smacked you in the teeth.' She slammed the window, picked up the bedroom extension and called the police.

It was one a.m. before local police, reinforced by officers from Bury St Edmunds, were able to persuade the invaders to depart and let the Ryes get some sleep. Even then, most of them didn't go far. Every room at every inn for kilometres around was occupied by journalists, and some of those who failed to find accommodation slept in their vehicles, so that when Kizzy peeped out at eight after a restless night, there were men on the lawn.

TWENTY-SEVEN

'No school today, my darlings,' smiled Harper as her dazed children trailed down to breakfast. 'Can't have you running the gauntlet of those vultures out there, and anyway it's ten past eight now – we'd never make it.'

'I'm glad,' yawned Frazer. 'I didn't fancy facing everybody today – people at school, I mean. Not if we're in the papers.'

Kizzy shook her head. 'Me neither. I've been thinking about that man. He might be after me again because we spoiled his story.'

They were halfway through breakfast when the phone rang. 'Oh, no,' groaned Harper. 'This makes four times this morning.' She got up. Kizzy expected her to start yelling at the caller but instead she sighed and relaxed against the wall, smiling. 'Oh, it's *you*, Hazel. Thank goodness. I thought – yes, yes, it's me all right. Us, I should say. We're besieged, my love. Trapped in our own home. What're they saying about us, anyway? Oh yes, I can imagine. Well – that's very kind, Hazel, and it'd be lovely to see you, but I wouldn't if I were you. You'd be mobbed – dragged from your vehicle and scragged before you could say "no comment". Well, if you're absolutely sure— You're a hero, darling, I've always said so. We'll keep the coffee on and man the door. Yes. Yes, we look forward to that. 'Bye.'

'Hazel's coming,' stated Frazer as his mother sat down.

Harper nodded. 'She is, the intrepid fool, *and* she's bringing the morning papers which are absolutely black with inaccurate headlines about us. We must be ready to let her in the instant she arrives.'

Hazel Ratcliffe lived and worked in Ipswich, and it was after ten when her Euro came bouncing up the driveway, pursued by four men on foot. As the car

87

pulled up by the front door, Frazer flung it open and yelled, 'This way, Hazel – quick!'

It was a desperately close thing. As the lecturer scuttled into the hallway with a wodge of newspapers under her arm, a camera flashed. Frazer was momentarily blinded, and when he went to slam the door there was a foot in it. '*Aaaagh!*' The reporter screamed, snatched back his crushed foot and hopped about on the step, nursing it. When Frazer slammed the door it hit him a terrific blow on the ear. He toppled, rolled down the steps and lay sobbing at the feet of his slower colleagues. Kizzy, who had watched the whole thing through a curtained window, laughed maliciously and let the curtain fall.

TWENTY-EIGHT

'So let's have a look at what they're saying.' Harper slid a tabloid from the top of the pile while Hazel sipped coffee. Kizzy and Frazer peered at the head-line over their mother's shoulder.

'DOCTOR WHO?' it bellowed.

'Oh, no,' groaned Harper for the second time that morning. She skimmed the story, threw the paper aside and reached for another.

'SUFFOLK MUM CLAIMS TARDIS BREAK-THROUGH!' it read. 'Copycat!' scoffed Harper.

'How about this?' Frazer grabbed a tabloid and read out: 'SUFFOLK HUNCH: BOFFIN'S TIME BREAKTHROUGH.'

'Oh, Lord!' sighed Harper. 'What an *excruciating* pun. Let's have another, quick.' She snatched one from the pile.

'SINGLE MUM IN CETACEAN RELO-CATION SENSATION,' this one read, over a picture of the unfortunate whale. Harper laughed.

'Really imaginative effort from the *Financial Times*,' chuckled Hazel, pouring more coffee. 'TIME-TRAVEL CLAIM – MARKETS CAUTIOUS.'

Kizzy picked up a broadsheet. 'This one's different, Mum. It sounds foreign. Listen. KRA S'HAON SM.'

'Eh?' Frazer peered at the headline. 'KRA S'HAON SM? What the heck does that mean, Mum?'

Harper took the paper from Kizzy and studied the headline, frowning. Then her brow cleared and she chuckled. 'That's quite clever, I suppose. Try it backwards, darling.'

Kizzy's lips moved as she read the headline from right to left. A smile dawned. 'MS NOAH'S ARK,' she murmured. 'It *is* good, isn't it, in a way?'

'*I* don't think so,' growled Frazer. 'How many

people're going to try it backwards? They'll think it's gobbledygook.'

His mother shook her head. 'I doubt it, darling. That paper's famous for its crossword. I fancy most of its readers will spot the reversal pretty quickly. After all, it's only an anagram.'

'Well.' Hazel put down her cup and smiled. 'How does it feel to hit the headlines, folks?'

Harper grimaced. 'It's not the headlines that worry me, Hazel, it's the stories underneath. So much sensation, so few facts. I'm afraid—'

'Hey, Mum.' Kizzy was by the window. 'They're all going away – look.'

It was true. The yard was emptying. Only a three-man camera crew remained, dismantling its equipment. Frazer ran to the living-room, peered into the garden and yelled, 'It's the same this side, Mum. They're going.'

'Hooray!' cried Kizzy. 'We're free. We can go anywhere we like. Hey, Mum – Hazel – how about a picnic in the woods to celebrate?'

'Good idea,' laughed Hazel, but Harper didn't respond. She was gazing through the window at a man standing in the gateway. She was sure she'd seen him before. He was watching the cars and vans depart. When the last one had gone, he turned to look at the house and she remembered who he was. 'Mr Morton,' she murmured.

'What?' queried Kizzy.

'Mr Morton's here,' said Harper. 'Morton of the M.o.D. I think our picnic might have to wait a while.'

TWENTY-NINE

'This press release,' said Morton, when he and Harper were alone in the living-room. 'Is there any truth in it?'

Harper gazed at him. 'Of course. I told you when you came before but you refused to listen. How did you get rid of the media?'

'I'll ask the questions if you don't mind, Doctor Rye. So that's how you got hold of those red kites – with your time machine?'

Harper nodded. 'I prefer to call it Rye's Apparatus, Mr Morton. Time machine sounds so sci-fi, don't you think?'

The man shrugged. 'The name is immaterial, Doctor Rye. The point is that if your claim is true, you have invented a device with immense potential and to go to the Press the way you did was an act of gross irresponsibility. Foreign powers will have been alerted. They may well wish to possess your – apparatus. Did that possibility not occur to you?'

Harper nodded. 'Mr Morton, I am well aware that there are unscrupulous people who will use any new invention for their own ends, but it was a risk I had to take for the sake of my children. We were being hounded by the tabloids. As far as I'm concerned, my apparatus is a device for reintroducing to the Earth plants and animals which we have wiped out with our thoughtlessness and our greed. Used responsibly, it can only be a good thing. It is *not* a weapon.'

Morton frowned. 'Unfortunately, Doctor, that is not for you to decide. If your apparatus has military potential, your country will want to exploit it. It's as simple as that.' He stood up. 'Show it to me.'

Suppressing her anger, the physicist led Morton to the room at the end of the house which served as her laboratory. She unlocked the door and stood aside to let him enter. 'There. That's my apparatus.'

Morton gazed at the gleaming ring of micro-circuitry in the middle of the room. 'Good Lord,' he breathed. 'And it really works, eh?'

Harper made no reply. She was trying to imagine how this man and those like him might twist her invention into a killing machine. There was no doubt in her mind that they'd manage it.

'And what's that?' Morton nodded towards the console which occupied all of one wall.

'That's my control centre,' said Harper. 'It's basically a linked series of computers. Would you like me to demonstrate?'

He looked at her. 'Capture something from the past, you mean? Bring it here, now?'

Harper nodded. 'That's what it does.'

He hesitated, drawing his tongue along his lower lip. Then, reluctantly it seemed, he shook his head. 'No – that won't be necessary, thank you.' He cleared his throat. 'Soon, our people will come and remove this apparatus to one of our evaluation centres. At that stage you may well be required to demonstrate, and to advise. In the meantime I would urge you to keep the device, together with any papers pertaining to it, totally—'

'Hey, just a minute!' cried Harper. 'This is *my* apparatus you're talking about. It's *mine*. How d'you mean, *our people will come and remove it*? You can't just—'

Morton stared at her, unblinking. 'Oh, but we can, Doctor Rye. I promise you, we can.'

'What about the Press, then? *They'll* be back the minute you leave, wanting to know—'

Morton shook his head. 'The Press won't bother you again.' He smiled a brief, tight smile. 'That's another promise.'

He didn't stay for the coffee Harper offered, and she was glad. She'd offered it out of politeness, but it had felt like offering hospitality to a burglar. When he'd gone, and Hazel asked if she was feeling all right, she surprised herself by flinging her arms round her friend and bursting into tears.

THIRTY

'Do we *have* to go today, Mum – can't we wait till Monday?' Kizzy had on her best pleading look, but Harper was adamant.

'You have to get it over with, darling, and it would feel just as difficult on Monday as it does today.' She smiled. 'Anyway, it won't be half as bad as you think it's going to be – things never are.'

'Huh – you don't know the kids, Mum. They'll be there already, waiting to pounce.'

'Yeah,' nodded Frazer. 'At my place, too. That Sefton.'

All arguments proved futile. At eight o'clock, brother and sister were in the Suzuki with their bags between their feet, and Harper was steering the vehicle out of the driveway.

She dropped them at around eight-thirty and set off back, unsure of what her next move ought to be. There was the white-headed duck, of course – a recently extinct bird she'd intended snatching from the nineteen nineties – but Morton and the Press had unsettled her. Especially Morton, whom she found sinister in spite of his grey suit and quiet way of speaking. Or perhaps *because* of them.

She was thinking about Morton as she swung the Suzuki on to the rough track which led to the house, and she didn't notice the girl till it was almost too late. She gasped and stood on the brake, bringing the vehicle to a screeching halt. The girl stood in the middle of the track, gazing in at her as though nothing had happened. Harper, shaken and furious, wound down her window.

'What the devil do you think you're doing?' she snapped. 'Do you realize I almost killed you just now?'

The girl smiled dreamily. 'That would've been all right – I'd be with *him*, you see – for ever.' As the girl spoke, two others emerged from the shrubs and stood behind her, and Harper noticed they all wore the same T-shirts.

'What are you talking about, you silly girl? You don't *want* to die, surely?'

The girl shook her head. 'Not if *he* can live again.'

'He?' cried Harper. 'Who's this *he* you keep mentioning?'

The girl smiled again. 'Vulcan Pan, of course. The most fantastic guy who ever lived. He was God, you know.'

'Vulcan—? Ah, right.' Harper nodded. Vulcan Pan, the pop star. Frazer had been keen on him a couple of years back. She looked at the girl. 'But he's – he's dead, isn't he? A car crash or something.'

The girl shook her head. 'Not to us, he's not. Look.' She opened her jacket to reveal the words on her T-shirt. VULCAN PAN LIVES. She gazed at the physicist with shining eyes. 'We stayed faithful, you see, and now we know why. We were chosen – *he* chose us to come to you and fix his resurrection.'

'Fix his— Oh, no.' Harper shook her head. 'No, no, no. No, you've made a mistake, my dear, believe me. I can't – it's impossible, that's all. Quite impossible.'

'Oh no, it's not.' The girl's eyes filled with tears. 'Don't say that to us. Not to *us*. We stayed faithful all this time, and it was for *this*. It was for *you*. We were waiting – *he* was waiting – for you. Don't you *see*?'

Harper shook her head. She felt sick. The Suzuki's engine had stalled when she braked. She restarted it and called over its growl, 'Go away, please. I really am most terribly sorry, but I can't help you and you must leave. This is a private track and you're trespassing.' She released the brake and the Suzuki rolled forward. At the last possible moment the girls stepped aside, their faces streaked with tears. Harper kept her gaze fixed straight ahead but she could feel their eyes on her, and when she drew level, the girl who had spoken spat through the open window and cried, 'We *won't* leave, d'you hear? We'll *camp* here till you change your mind. *He'll* come to you. *He'll* make you do what we want!'

Harper drove on, wiping spittle from her cheek with the back of her hand.

THIRTY-ONE

'Look out, guys – here comes Doctor Who!' Ashley Hallas pointed as Frazer walked into the yard. Kids, yelling and cheering, converged on their victim so that he found himself in the middle of a jostling scrum.

'Hey, Rye!' shouted someone. 'Get us a whale.'

'Yeah!' cried another. 'Dump it in the assembly hall – close the school.'

'What about a Bengal tiger for the Head's bedroom?' suggested a girl.

'And a fistful of newts in old Ibbotson's knickers!'

demanded another. Ms Ibbotson taught Biology.

'OK, OK,' grinned Frazer. 'I knew it was going to be like this. All suggestions will be given careful consideration, as the Chairman of Governors might say, but I'm making no promises.' Ironic cheers greeted this pronouncement. Frazer surveyed the crowd. 'Anybody seen Bilbo this morning?'

'I have,' volunteered Hallas. 'Shall I tell him a Time Lord wants to see him?'

'Tell him nothing,' growled Frazer. 'Where is he?'

'He *was* skulking behind the toolshed, scoffing a choc bar. Someone seems to have left him a million E or something – he's spending it like water these days.'

Andrew Baggins was stuffing the remains of a Snickers bar into his face when Frazer found him. He didn't seem pleased to see his friend.

'Whaddya want?' he grunted, through a cud of sugary goo.

'Nothing *you've* got, you rotten little plonker,' snarled Frazer. 'You were a guest in our home and you spied on us.'

'Howdya mean?' Brown spit oozed from a corner of Bilbo's mouth and trickled down his chin.

'You went snooping around the place, trying to find out about my mother's work even though I told you it was hush-hush, and then you spilled your guts to some media-creep who threatened my sister and forced Mum to go public.' He grabbed a handful of the boy's shirt and tie. 'How much did he pay you, Baggins?'

'N-nothing,' spluttered Bilbo. 'Honest.'

'Did it for love, did you?'

'Yes. I mean, no. It was scientific enquiry, Frazer. People have a right to know.'

'Right to know, you sanctimonious little twerp?' Frazer tightened his grip and lifted Bilbo off his feet. The boy's face reddened and his eyes goggled as Frazer's fist closed his airway. He gasped, dribbling liquified Snickers down his face. Frazer used his free hand to scrape up a palmful of the mess, which he then proceeded to smear over every part of Bilbo's face and into his ears. He ended by rubbing the stuff vigorously into the boy's hair before letting him fall to the ground, where he lay sniffling.

Frazer was washing his hands in the cloakroom when the buzzer signalled the start of the school day and Stanton Sefton sidled up to him. 'Hey, Rye,' he murmured. 'Your mum picks you up after school, right?'

'Right.'

'Well, my dad wants to talk to her. He'll be by the gate at half-past three.'

'OK. I'm not sure she'll talk to him, though.'

Sefton chuckled nastily and ruffled Frazer's hair. 'Oh, she'll talk to him all right, kiddo,' he said. 'People usually do what my dad wants.' He walked on.

Frazer gazed after him. He'd felt good after his session with Bilbo, but he didn't feel so good now.

THIRTY-TWO

A ring of children held hands and danced round Kizzy, chanting, 'a panda, a panda, a panda!'

'I can't. It isn't *like* that. Mum's not in the *pets* trade. Her animals are for releasing into the wild.' Her words were disregarded – drowned out by the chanting. She wished the bell would go.

'Leave her alone!'

Kizzy's heart soared as Jennifer Stone appeared, fighting to break the circle, tugging it out of shape as she hauled on a boy's arm. Kizzy charged the same boy who, finding himself under attack from front and rear, relinquished his grip on his friends' hands and whirled, ready to defend himself. As he did so, Gabrielle Kromer arrived, flinging herself at the girl next to him. The circle disintegrated as its members, out for fun but not for a fight, scattered. In a moment the three girls found themselves in possession of this bit of the playground.

'Thanks,' breathed Kizzy. 'That chanting was starting to do my head in.'

'Any time,' grinned Gabrielle. 'Nothing like a good scrap to set you up for the day, is there, Jenny?'

Jennifer, who hated fighting, smiled and looked down. The three friends drifted towards the building in anticipation of the bell.

At the end of assembly Mr Donovan said, 'I want to see Kizzy Rye in my room right away, please.'

Kizzy swallowed. Kids were whispering – turning round to look at her. She felt her cheeks going red.

'Now, Kizzy.' The Head gazed at her across his desk. 'I noticed a disturbance in the playground this morning. You seemed to be in the middle of it. What was it all about?'

'Sir, they—'

'Never mind *they*. What were *you* doing?'

'I – I was trying to tell them, sir.'

'Tell them what?'

'That my mother can't get them a panda, sir.'

'A panda? What on earth are you talking about, Kizzy Rye?'

'Sir, they think I can get them a panda with my mother's apparatus. I was trying to explain—'

'Ah, yes.' Mr Donovan nodded. 'Your mother's apparatus. Now we're coming to it.'

'Pardon, sir?'

'I said we were coming to it, Kizzy. The heart of the matter. I read the papers too, you know.'

'Yes, sir.'

'Yes, sir.' He nodded, regarding Kizzy from beneath his bushy eyebrows. 'Fame, Kizzy. Or notoriety. Mustn't get carried away by it must we, hmm? Mustn't let it go to our heads.'

'Sir, I'm *not*. I—'

'Don't *interrupt*, child. Don't *contradict*. Listen. I know you, Kizzy, as I know every child in my school. I watch you, you see. You've always been a quiet child. A good child. A hard worker who never makes a fuss. Then your mother gets her name in the papers and in no time at all you're causing disruption in the playground. It won't do, Kizzy, do you understand? I won't have it.'

'But, sir, I— It's not fair. I didn't start it. They were all waiting for me.'

'That will do, Kizzy. I'm not interested in excuses. Just remember what I've said. We don't have prima donnas at this school.'

'There's *one*.' She hadn't meant to say it. She was angry and it just slipped out. The Head's gaze was chilling.

'*What* did you say, Kizzy Rye?'

'Nothing, sir.'

'It didn't sound like nothing to me.' He stood up. 'I'm disappointed in you, Kizzy. Bitterly disappointed. I shall write to your mother. Go to your class now.'

Kizzy went to her class, but she did no work. She couldn't. Her mind kept going over the terrible thing she'd said to Mr Donovan – the letter her mother would get. 'I wish,' she whispered, over and over, 'I wish I'd never *heard* of Rye's Apparatus.'

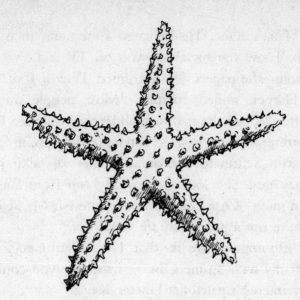

THIRTY-THREE

Harper lowered the Suzuki's window to watch the kids streaming through the gateway. She'd just spotted Frazer when a shadow fell across her and a man poked his head in.

'It's Doctor Rye, isn't it?'

'Yes.' Harper's tone was cautious. 'And this is my daughter, Kizzy.'

The man nodded. 'Hello, Kizzy.' He smiled briefly then looked at Harper. 'My name's Martin Sefton. My son's in Frazer's year.'

'Oh, yes. Frazer's mentioned him. Stanton, isn't it?'

'That's right.' He hesitated a moment, then went on. 'I saw the bit about you on TV and I've been reading the papers. I'm intrigued, Doctor Rye.'

Harper smiled ruefully. 'Most people are, Mr Sefton.' Over the man's shoulder she could see Frazer twirling a finger beside his temple then pointing it at Martin Sefton to indicate that she was talking to a crazy guy. She looked away to keep from laughing and said, 'What exactly is your interest, Mr Sefton – you're not a journalist, are you?'

'Oh no, nothing like that. I'm a heating engineer – run my own business. No – I suppose you could say my interest's patriotic, Doctor Rye.'

'Patriotic?'

'Yes. Things haven't been going too well with the old country lately, have they? Recession, violent crime, bombings, riots. People aren't safe on the streets any more.'

Harper nodded. 'True.'

'Ever wondered why?'

'I *know* why, Mr Sefton. There are no decent jobs. People are homeless. Conditions like these are bound to cause unrest.'

'No, no, Doctor.' The man shook his head vigorously. 'All that is incidental. What's wrong – what's *missing* – is strong leadership.'

'You think so?'

'I *know* so. What this country needs is a leader who sees what needs to be done and does it, no matter how unpopular it makes him. A man who doesn't *care* what people think.'

Harper shook her head. 'That doesn't sound like a very good idea to me, Mr Sefton. What you're describing is some sort of dictator, and anyway I don't see what all this has to do with my work, so if you'll excuse me I have to get my kids home.'

Sefton shook his head. 'Not *some sort* of dictator, Doctor Rye. I'm not talking about *some sort* of dictator. I'm talking about *the* dictator – the greatest man who ever lived. I'm talking about Adolf Hitler.'

'*Hitler?*' Harper laughed. 'You're insane, Mr Sefton. Adolf Hitler was responsible for more suffering than any single man before or since. He was nothing but a monster.' She peered over Sefton's shoulder and called, 'Frazer? Come along, darling – time to go.'

'Wait!' As she started the engine the man reached in and grabbed the wheel. 'We can bring him back. You and I. Bring him *here*. With his methods and the backing of the organization I belong to, he'd *transform* this country – turn it around. And it would all be down to you, Doctor Rye – you and your wonderful machine!'

Harper looked at the man. 'What exactly *is* this organization of yours, Mr Sefton?'

The man's smile was wolfish. 'The New Britain Movement, naturally. They're the only true patriots we have left in this country.'

'They're Nazis,' snarled Harper. 'A bunch of Nazi thugs who can't muster a decent brain between them. Take your hand off my wheel, please – we're going.'

Frazer was clambering into the Suzuki. Sefton retained his grip. 'Listen,' he hissed. 'The NBM will do anything for England, Doctor Rye – *anything*.' He was forced to let go of the wheel as the Suzuki rolled forward. 'You'll get a visit from us one of these nights – you can depend on it. Nobody says no to me.'

'I *told* you he was nuts,' chuckled Frazer as they pulled away. 'It runs in the family.'

'It's not *funny*!' cried Kizzy. 'I got in trouble today because of all this and it wasn't my fault. I wish we could just go away and forget all about it.'

'I'm sorry,' sighed Harper. 'Really I am.' She was thinking about the pop fans waiting by the gateway at home. 'I'll get us out of this, darlings, I promise. Somehow, I'll get us out.'

She wished she felt as confident as she sounded.

THIRTY-FOUR

The fans were waiting. They'd constructed a bender
– a shelter made from saplings and polythene – among
the shrubs just outside the gateway. As the Suzuki came
bouncing down the track, they emerged from this and
linked arms, blocking the way. There were five of them
now.

'What the heck's *this*?' cried Frazer.

'Sorry, darlings,' muttered Harper, hitting the brake
and the horn at the same time. 'It's the Vulcan
Pan fan club. They want me to snatch their hero
– resurrect him, as they put it.'

'I don't believe it.'

As the vehicle squealed to a stop, the young women broke their chain and surrounded it, rapping on windows, pressing their faces against the glass, chanting. One girl leant across the bonnet and held a sheet of paper to the windscreen. On it, in green felt-tip, were the words:

YOUR DESTINY YOU CAN'T DENY –
BRING BACK OUR VULCAN, DOCTOR
RYE

'My God,' breathed Frazer. 'They're even nuttier than Martin Sefton. What're you going to *do*, Mum?'

'Creep forward, I suppose,' said Harper. 'Very slowly, and hope they don't attack with stones or something.' She blipped the horn and eased the Suzuki forward at five kilometres an hour. The fans kept pace, pounding on the roof with their fists and pulling such hideous faces that Kizzy closed her eyes. As the vehicle began to pass between the gateposts, they fell away and stood in a sullen knot, watching it recede. There were no stones, and no more spittle.

'Are we getting the police?' asked Frazer, as his mother drew up by the door. 'They'll soon shift 'em.'

Harper shook her head. 'I don't think so, dear. They're seriously mixed up but I doubt if they're dangerous. It's that Sefton character *I'm* worried about.'

The fans chanted steadily through the evening, forcing the Ryes to keep the windows closed and drown them out with TV. It was after ten when the noise finally stopped and the two youngsters went to bed. Harper switched off the television and sat in the dark, wrestling with the problem of what to do. Used as she'd intended, Rye's Apparatus was harmless. In fact, it was positively beneficial, yet already there were people out there who wanted it used in other ways – to alter human history and to hurt others. Some of them were crazy, of course, and they could probably be coped with, but what about the M.o.D.? Morton wasn't crazy, yet he and people like him seemed intent on using her invention as a weapon.

Lost in thought, she didn't notice the time till a knock on the door made her jump. She glanced at the clock and frowned. Twenty to twelve. Who on earth would be knocking at this time of night? Martin Sefton, said a little voice in her head. Martin Sefton *and friends*. She got up and tiptoed to a window from which she could see the door.

It was a man, but not Sefton and not, from the look of him, one of Sefton's friends. He was a short, elderly, sad-looking man with glasses and sparse white hair. He was wearing a shabby raincoat and shuffling about in the glare of the security lamp, looking this way and that as though wondering whether to try another knock. Harper let the curtain fall and went to the door which she opened on its chain, peering through the narrow slot.

'Yes?'

'Oh – good evening.' The caller seemed nervous. Apologetic.

'Good evening,' returned Harper, briskly. 'How may I help you?'

The man smiled diffidently. 'I – I'm sorry to be calling at this late hour, Doctor Rye. I wasn't sure you'd still be up.'

'No, well – it's a wonder I am. What can I do for you?'

The man glanced over his shoulder. 'Do you think I might come in for a moment? There are some people by your gate. Young people. They make me nervous.'

'Of course.' She slipped the chain and opened the door. 'Though it *is* very late and I was just going to bed.'

'I know, I'm very sorry.' The man scurried forward and wiped his shoes on the mat.

Harper closed and locked the door and looked at him enquiringly. 'Now, what is it?'

'It's my wife.' There was a catch in his voice as he said this.

'Your wife?'

'Yes.'

'What about your wife, Mr – er—?'

'Lawson. Albert Lawson. She died, you see.'

'I'm sorry, Mr Lawson.'

The man nodded. 'Yes. It's been almost a year now.'

'A year,' echoed Harper. She didn't know what else to say. A horrible presentiment was forming in her mind.

'Almost a year, and I can't get over it. People – friends – keep telling me it'll get better, but it doesn't.' He looked up at the physicist, his eyes brimming with tears. 'I can't live without her, Doctor, that's the truth of the matter. I want her back, and when I read about you in the paper I knew I had to come and see you.'

'Mr Lawson.' He was weeping now, bent over, his face buried in his hands. 'Mr Lawson, I think I know why you've come, and believe me I'd give anything to be able to help you, but I can't.'

'Can't?' Lawson lifted his head. 'Of course you can. If it works with animals, it must work with people. All you have to do is—'

'It's not that simple,' said Harper, as gently as she could. 'Snatching an animal – even an insect

117

– alters history, but in a way that is unlikely to make a significant difference. Snatching a *person* – resurrecting them, in effect – is a different matter entirely. It could have catastrophic consequences. I can't do it, Mr Lawson.'

The man bit his lip, fighting to control his tears. His features shifted, grief giving way to angry scepticism. 'I don't care about history, Doctor Rye,' he croaked. 'All I know is, you have the ability to give me back my wife. You can see the state I'm in. What sort of person would refuse to help a fellow creature in distress, eh – what sort of person?'

'My God!' Harper gazed at him. 'Don't you think there are people *I'd* give anything to have with me again? I had parents, Mr Lawson. Grandparents. A baby who died in her cot. I have the ability to bring *them* back too, but I don't. I haven't. I'm a scientist, Mr Lawson. I have responsibilities.'

'Yes.' The man's voice oozed bitterness. 'You're a scientist all right. A hard, unfeeling scientist, like those who made the atom bomb. You don't care any more about human suffering than *they* did.'

'They cared,' cried Harper. 'They split the atom – they didn't know others would use their work to make a bomb. We can never tell what use our discoveries will be put to, but we have to go on making them – it's our *job*.'

'Don't talk to me,' Lawson shook his head, 'because I don't want to hear anything you've got to say. Open the door and let me out, you heartless monster – I wish I'd never come.'

Harper couldn't watch his departure. She stood aside as he scurried by without so much as a glance at her, then closed the door and slumped against it, weeping.

THIRTY-FIVE

There were five items of mail that Friday morning. Harper brought them to the table and slit the envelopes while Frazer and Kizzy ate cornflakes. One envelope was addressed in green ink.

'Oh-oh,' went Harper.

Kizzy looked at her. 'What's wrong, Mum?'

Harper held up the envelope. 'Green ink. Sign of eccentricity.'

'I didn't know that. Open it – I could do with a good laugh.'

Harper pulled out the letter, smoothed it on the tablecloth and read. Kizzy and Frazer watched her. When she got to the end she chuckled and shook her head. 'Unbelievable.'

'What?' asked Frazer.

'It's from the Friends of Tyrannosaurus Rex.'

'What – the old rock band?'

'No, darling – the even older gigantic lizard.'

'The *dinosaur?*' cried Kizzy.

Harper nodded. 'Listen.' She read aloud.

Dear Doctor Rye,

    You don't know me. My name's Danvers Peterson and I'm Secretary of an organization called Friends of Tyrannosaurus Rex. We read about you in the paper and we had an idea. You've got children so you'll know how kids are fascinated by dinosaurs. What if some people got together and built a THEME PARK with REAL dinosaurs in their natural habitat? All we'd need would be a few acres of scrub with perhaps a swampy bit, and you could get the right plants – giant tree-ferns and so on – and the actual dinosaurs. People would flock in their thousands to see it. We'd stand to make a fortune. Of course, we realize we'd have to be careful about security – wouldn't do to have dinosaurs rampaging about the countryside (ha ha!) – but we can cross that bridge when we come to it. My friends and I would pay for the land and see to all the work. What do you think? Looking forward to hearing from you soon.

Yours hopefully.

'Sounds great,' grinned Frazer. 'I can't *wait* to clean up after something that eats a tonne and a half of Kit-E-Kat a day.'

'Trust you to think of something like *that*,' said Kizzy. She looked at her mother. 'Can Rye's Apparatus go back that far, Mum?'

Harper nodded. 'Oh, yes. Theoretically there's no limit, but of course the theme-park idea's ridiculous. In fact,' she smiled, 'there was a film – oh, forty years ago – about this very thing. I saw a clip on TV not so long ago. I wouldn't be surprised if that's where these airheads got the idea from.'

'Will you write and tell this Peterson character it's not on?' asked Frazer.

Harper sighed. 'I don't think so, darling. I've enough to think about without responding to screwball letters in green ink.' She drained her coffee cup and stood up. 'Come on – let's get the two of you to school.'

'Er – hmm,' went Kizzy. 'Talking of letters and school—'

Her mother looked at her. 'What is it, darling?'

Kizzy told about her interview the previous day with Mr Donovan. 'So you'll get another nutty letter tomorrow,' she concluded. 'Sorry.'

Harper shook her head. 'It seems to me that Mr Donovan picked on you unfairly, though of course you certainly ought not to have said what you said to him. I'll pop in with you this morning and have a quiet word.'

'Oh, terrific,' groaned Kizzy. 'That's all I need. He'll probably hang me in assembly or something.'

'If he does,' grinned Frazer, 'can I have the dosh out of your piggy-bank?'

THIRTY-SIX

Andrew Baggins lived only a couple of kilometres from school, so unless the weather was foul he biked it. It wasn't foul that Friday morning and that was bad luck for Bilbo, because Harvey Parvin was waiting in his Mazda on the one quiet stretch of the boy's route. As Bilbo pedalled towards the car it pulled across the narrow lane, blocking it. Parvin opened his door as the bike wobbled to a stop.

'Morning, Bilbo.'

'Oh – er – morning. Did you want to see me?'

The journalist smiled like a crocodile. 'I will say to

you the word *discretion*, lad. Remember it, do you? We talked about it the last time we met.'

'Yes, I remember.'

'And what did discretion mean, Bilbo?'

'I – er – had to keep quiet about what I told you, and not ask questions, and not go near the Hammer and Anvil till I was eighteen.'

'Correct. So why did you go blabbering to every skunk and his uncle as soon as my back was turned?'

'I – I *didn't*. Honestly. I haven't said a word to anyone.'

'Rubbish, lad! When I left that pub, there was only you and me knew anything about what the Rye woman had been up to, yet a few hours later it was common knowledge. *I* didn't blab, so you must have.'

'But I *didn't*, Mr Parvin. I swear I didn't.'

'Don't give me that, son. I paid for exclusive information and you promptly flogged it elsewhere. You owe me fifty E.'

'But I haven't *got* it, Mr Parvin. I spent it.'

'Ah!' Parvin's expression was grave. 'That puts you in big trouble, my son. *Big* trouble.'

'W-what d'you mean?' Bilbo glanced about him, hoping someone would appear. The journalist closed his door and spoke through the open window. 'Stay there. I'm going to re-park this thing, then you and I must have a little talk. Oh – and don't think about pedalling off, Bilbo old lad. Kids have been known to get knocked down in country lanes. Happens all the time.'

Bilbo leaned his bike on the hedge as Parvin parked the Mazda. He considered dashing off into the trees, but the man looked fit enough to outrun him and Bilbo decided he'd rather talk to him at the roadside than in the middle of a thicket.

'Right, now.' Parvin rubbed his hands together. 'About this fifty E.'

'I told you, Mr Parvin, I haven't got it. There was this microscope, second hand—'

'I'm not interested in your shopping, son. I want my money. If you don't have it, you'll just have to work it off.'

'Work it off? What d'you mean?'

The journalist shrugged. 'It's perfectly simple. You owe me fifty ecu. You don't have the cash, so you do fifty E's worth of work for me and we're straight.'

'W-what sort of work?'

'Oh - nothing you'd need a university education to do, Bilbo old son. You'd take a few snapshots, that's all.'

'Snapshots?'

'That's right. Got a camera, have you?'

'Yes. A Minolta. What d'you want me to photograph?'

126

'Rye's Apparatus.'

'But I – the apparatus must be inside the house, Mr Parvin. I've looked in all the outhouses and it wasn't there. I can't go into that house any more. The Ryes hate me for talking to you. Frazer roughed me up.'

The man shrugged. 'You've stayed there. You know the layout. Find a way in. You've no choice. A debt's a debt, and you wouldn't believe how nasty I can get with little boys who don't pay their debts.'

'All right, I'll try,' mumbled Bilbo miserably. 'When d'you want it done?'

'Sooner the better.'

'And how do I contact you?'

'You don't. I'll be watching. When you've done it, I'll contact you.' He glanced at his watch. 'You'd better be off or you'll be late. Ta-ta for now, Bilbo.'

Bilbo mounted and rode on. He felt as though someone had piled a tonne of scrap iron on his shoulders. Just before the bend, he glanced back. Parvin was standing on the same spot, gazing after him.

THIRTY-SEVEN

'Frazer darling.' Harper looked across the table at her son. 'I want you to do something for me.'

'What is it, Mum?' He was playing with the food on his plate. The square of quiche was the house. He'd surrounded it with a rampart of mashed potato. The peas round the rim of the plate were Martin Sefton and his friends, trying to get in.

'I don't like the idea of leaving this place empty tomorrow. I want you to stay at home while Kizzy and I go into town.'

'Aw, Mu-um!' whinged Frazer. 'We always go

together. I've arranged to meet Ashley and some of the others in the Arndale to look at CDs.'

'I *know* it's inconvenient, dear, but you could phone Ashley, tell him you can't make it.' She smiled. 'It really *would* set my mind at rest.'

'Oh, all right.' He placed a particularly large pea beside the quiche to represent himself. 'At least I'll get a lie-in.'

THIRTY-EIGHT

Bilbo got very little sleep that Friday night. As soon as he lay down in bed the tonne of scrap iron on his shoulders transferred itself to the middle of his chest, making it difficult to breathe. He lay sweating, staring up into a blackness in which phantom lights floated.

He wished he'd never heard of Frazer Rye. He regretted having stayed with the Ryes at Christmas. He wished he'd minded his own business while he was there. Most of all, he wished he hadn't contacted Harvey Parvin.

Fifty E. Can they put you in prison for owing

somebody fifty ecu? Bilbo didn't know, but he knew they could put you there for breaking into somebody's house. Perhaps he should take a chance – refuse to do what Parvin wanted and hope the journalist wouldn't get him jailed. Yeah, that's it! he thought. He felt the scrap iron getting lighter. I won't do it. I just won't. I bet he can't get me for it. He smiled into the darkness as the weight floated away. He rolled on to his side and closed his eyes.

Bilbo was almost asleep when he remembered the film. It was a film he'd watched on telly the week before, about a woman who gambled on horse-races. She couldn't help it. She put all her money on horses – all the housekeeping and everything – and when that was gone she borrowed from a money-lender so that she could keep on gambling. It was a sad film, but the bit Bilbo was remembering was more scary than sad. It was the bit where the woman couldn't pay back the money-lender, and the money-lender got nasty. He didn't call the police and try to get the woman jailed or anything. Instead, he paid two thugs to ambush her one night and break both her legs.

Both her legs. Bilbo rolled on to his back and groaned. I *knew* Harvey Parvin reminded me of someone, he whispered. Now I remember. The money-lender. He looks just like the actor who played the money-lender in the film. What if – what if he doesn't even *try* to get me jailed for his rotten fifty E? What if he gets a couple of big rough guys to wait for me after school and break my legs? Come to think of it, it wouldn't even take two *big* guys – two average guys would do. Or one.

So. He stared at the ceiling. I'm going to have to do it, and I know how, he thought. The window in the guest bedroom has a broken catch and there's a set of ladders in one of the outbuildings. That's how.

And I know when. Saturdays, the Ryes come into Bury St Edmunds. All of 'em. Frazer meets some of the guys. Kizzy has a dancing class. Their mother shops. They have lunch in town, get home around two-thirty, three o'clock. I know all this 'cos Frazer told me. They don't have a dog, thank God, so why not tomorrow? Get it over with.

He groaned as the tonne weight settled once more in the middle of his chest.

THIRTY-NINE

There's nothing like a good lie-in on a Saturday morning after a hard week at school. This week had been particularly hard, what with one thing and another, and Frazer was still luxuriating in a delicious doze at ten o'clock, a full hour and a half after Kizzy and his mother had set off to Bury St Edmunds. He'd probably have kept it going for another hour or so, but in a moment of half-waking he heard an unusual sound.

It was a scraping, rattling noise. It didn't remind him of anything so he told himself it wasn't anything and rolled over, but he couldn't doze off again. A little voice in his head whispered, Hey, aren't you supposed to be on guard? Isn't that why you're here and not in town? He tried pulling the duvet up over his ears but he could still hear the noise, which seemed to be coming from the other side of the house — from the yard perhaps. He was thoroughly awake now, so he sat up and listened.

It *was* coming from the yard. It sounded like something being dragged across the cobbles. Something heavy. He got out of bed and went out on to the landing. As he did so, there came a sound he recognized. It was the solid clunk you get when a ladder is set against a house wall.

Frazer gulped. He hadn't *really* expected anyone to try breaking in while the others were away, but why else would someone put a ladder against the house? No window-cleaner ever came here, and his mother hadn't ordered any work done as far as he knew. Somebody was climbing the ladder now. The sound seemed to be coming from the spare bedroom.

A weapon. He needed a weapon. If he was to repel Martin Sefton, he'd have to be armed. Sefton was a nutcase, like his son. A dangerous nutcase. There was a gun — an ancient sporting gun — on the wall above the fireplace in the living-room. It had been there since before the Ryes moved in and was almost certainly useless, but maybe the sight of it would persuade the climber to retreat.

Frazer scampered down the stairs and into the living-room. He grabbed the gun and bounded back up, panting and cursing. The guy was at the window now – he heard the squeak of it opening. With what he hoped was a blood-curdling yell, he charged into the room, brandishing the gun. Andrew Baggins had one foot on the ladder and the other hooked over the sill. As the demented gunman appeared he tried to withdraw, but his jeans-leg snagged the faulty catch. In trying to jerk it free, the boy flung himself backwards, lost his foothold on the ladder and fell, striking his head on the cobbles. Frazer had recognized the intruder, but his relief turned to horror when he leaned out and saw his schoolmate lying still. He flung the gun on the bed, ran into his mother's room and grabbed the phone.

FORTY

'An ambulance is on its way.'

'Th-thanks.' Frazer replaced the receiver and stood for a moment gazing down at it, thinking. What do I do in the meantime? Is this vehicle coming from Bury St Edmunds or Ipswich or Timbuctoo? How long will it take to get here? He wondered if he ought to call the doctor, but that seemed daft when he'd already sent for an ambulance. He ran downstairs and out into the yard, hoping to find Bilbo sitting up, rubbing his head and saying, Where am I? or What happened? or something, but the boy lay motionless, curled round the foot of the ladder with a bubble of blood at the corner of his mouth.

Frazer felt helpless. He wanted to do something, but the only thing he could remember about first aid was that if the patient's air passage was clear, he shouldn't be moved till qualified help arrived. He knelt on the cobbles and put his ear to Bilbo's half-open mouth. The boy was breathing, though shallowly. Thank God for that, anyway.

Frazer got up and tried to look at his watch. He wasn't wearing it, and it was then he realized he was barefoot and in his pyjamas. Remembering the pop fans, he glanced towards the gate, and was relieved to find that nobody seemed to have seen him. He felt he ought not to leave Bilbo, but on the other hand what good was he doing? He hurried indoors, praying the ambulance would come while he was dressing.

It didn't. It had taken him less than five minutes to get his clothes on and drag a comb through his hair and, when he got outside, Bilbo seemed exactly the same. Frazer began to pace, looking from the gateway to his watch to the gateway again. 'Come *on*,' he whispered, over and over. 'For Pete's sake, come *on*.' He wished he'd noted the time when he made the nine-nine-nine call, but he hadn't. He wondered what you do if someone stops breathing. He felt sick, scared and utterly useless.

It seemed hours till he heard the siren, though in fact no more than fifteen minutes had elapsed since his call. Thankfully, he watched the two paramedics stretcher Bilbo into their vehicle.

'Is he going to be all right?' he asked.

The man nodded. 'I shouldn't worry, son. Can you contact his next of kin – parents or whatever?'

'Y-yes, I guess so.'

'Good, tell 'em Ipswich General, will you?'

'Ipswich General? Sure.'

He didn't fancy it. What was he supposed to *say*, for Pete's sake? Oh, Mr Baggins, Frazer Rye here. I caught your son breaking into our house. Ran at him with a gun, knocked him clean off his ladder. He fell ten metres on to cobbles and they've carted him off to hospital, unconscious. How's *Mrs* Baggins?

As it turned out, it was Mrs Baggins who answered the phone. Frazer didn't mention any break-in. He told her there'd been an accident involving a ladder, that Bilbo was in hospital and that the paramedic had said there was no need to worry. He was afraid she'd start asking questions, but she didn't. She was obviously puzzled as to why her son had been at the Rye home, but she thanked him for letting her know and rang off.

Probably in the car and off to Ipswich already, thought Frazer. He wished his mother would come home.

FORTY-ONE

The fans of Vulcan Pan were undemonstrative when the Suzuki returned. Harper, not knowing they'd seen an ambulance come and go, was agreeably surprised, but the look on Frazer's face as he hurried out to meet her gave her a jolt.

'What is it, darling – has something happened?'

'You could say that, yes.' Briefly, he related the morning's events.

When he'd finished Harper said, 'I'll call the hospital, see how he is, then I think I'd better get down there. You two stay here and I'll call you, OK?'

It was twilight before the phone rang. Frazer picked up the receiver. 'Mum?'

'Yes, darling, it's me. Is everything all right?'

'Sure. How's Bilbo?'

'He's resting comfortably, as they say. He's concussed and has a broken collar bone, but he'll be fine.'

'Thank goodness for that. Are his folks there?'

Harper chuckled. 'Oh yes, they're here. Baggins senior was quite aggressive when I arrived – red-faced and spluttering, puffed up with indignation – you know the type. His son, injured on our property and all that. We'd be hearing from his solicitor and so forth.' She chuckled again. 'He went ape-shape when I told him his precious son had been breaking in. Refused to believe it, of course, but then Bilbo admitted it and he collapsed like a pricked balloon. Went all subdued. Asked me not to press charges.'

Frazer laughed. 'Bilbo's talking, then? Did he say *why* he was breaking in?'

'Yes. Apparently, he'd sold information to some journalist. A man called Harvey Parvin, who'd paid him fifty ecu and demanded it back when our story hit the front pages. Bilbo'd spent the money so Parvin threatened him – implied that if he didn't get photos of Rye's Apparatus something terrible would happen to him.'

'The rotten swine.'

'I know. Anyway, Bilbo's described the man and his car – number and everything – so I fancy he'll be getting a visit from the police.'

'Good. When're you coming home, Mum? Kizzy's crying for you.'

'I am *not*!' Frazer ducked as his sister's stuffed koala whizzed by his head.

'I'm setting off *now*, darling – you know how I hate hospitals. Put the kettle on, and don't tease your sister – I suspect this Parvin character had a go at her, too.'

FORTY-TWO

'Mr Parvin?'

It was Sunday evening, and the bar lounge of the Hammer and Anvil was busy. Harvey Parvin gazed up at the young man in the grey suit. 'Who wants to know?'

'I'm John Fletcher, Mr Parvin. Constable Fletcher if you prefer. Mind if I sit down?'

Parvin shrugged. 'Please yourself.'

'Thanks.' The constable sat. 'A quiet word, sir, if you don't mind. About a lad called Andrew Baggins.'

'Baggins?' The journalist took a sip of his pint. 'Never heard of him.'

'You sure, sir? Goes by the name of Bilbo, apparently.'

'Naw. Doesn't ring a bell, Constable. Should it?'

'I think so, sir. You spoke to him yesterday. Asked him to take some snapshots for you, to work off a debt.'

'Never.'

'He says you did, Mr Parvin. Says you scared him. He's in hospital because of you.'

'H-hospital?' Parvin slopped beer down his chin. 'Hey, just a minute – I'm not responsible for *anybody* being in hospital.'

'I think you are, sir. The kid was up a ladder, trying to break into the Rye place. He fell. You sent him there.'

'No way!' The journalist shook his head. 'I never told him to break in. That must've been his own idea.'

'So you *did* speak to him, sir?'

'Eh? Oh, all right – yes. I spoke to him. That's not an offence, is it?'

'Threatening behaviour is, Mr Parvin. You threatened the boy, didn't you?'

'I – he broke an agreement. I wanted my money back.'

143

'So you threatened him. You also threatened a little girl, Kizzy Rye.'

'How——? I never threatened her. I spoke to her, that's all.'

'You told her you might turn into one of those funny men her mum had warned her about. That's dodgy, Mr Parvin. Very dodgy. If I thought you were a man of that sort, I'd have to——'

'I'm not!' Parvin's hand was shaking so much he had to put down his glass. 'Look, Constable. I'm a journalist. All I ever wanted was information – a story. There's a magazine – a French magazine – they'd have paid a small fortune for those snapshots. I never meant to harm those kids – I've got two of my own, for heaven's sake.'

'Then take my advice, Mr Parvin. Go home to them. Leave Long Melford. Leave Suffolk. Go tonight. And if you ever feel tempted to come back, think about this – a woman who can dump a whale in a farmer's field might positively *enjoy* delivering a sabre-tooth tiger to a man who threatened her child.'

Harvey Parvin broke a number of speed records that night as he drove south-west through Ipswich, Colchester and Chelmsford, and it was more than a year before he stopped dreaming about the sabre-tooth tiger under his bed.

FORTY-THREE

'So this Parvin character's gone and the media's off our backs,' said Frazer. 'Things are looking up, eh, Mum?' It was Monday evening and Frazer was trying to cheer his mother up.

Harper smiled. 'You're an incurable optimist, darling, and I appreciate your efforts to lift me out of my depression, but I'm afraid it won't work. Parvin's gone, yes, and that's a good thing, but the M.o.D. scared the media away for its own reasons. Morton's pals will descend on us eventually, and God knows what will become of Rye's Apparatus then.'

'I wasn't teased at school today,' put in Kizzy. 'That's another good thing, isn't it?'

Harper smiled again. 'Of course it is, my love. Your mum's nothing but a miserable old sourpuss.'

'It's that man, isn't it?' said Frazer. 'The one who wants his wife back. That's what's *really* got to you.'

Harper nodded. 'Him, and those sad fans out there, and the Friends of Tyrannosaurus Rex, and the M.o.D. Not to mention poor Bilbo in hospital and Mad Martin Sefton.' She sighed. 'So many people, all anxious to use my invention in sick, wrong ways. And I'm afraid they will, in the end. Like Doctor Frankenstein, I've created something only to lose control of it.'

'We can snatch a few more creatures though, can't we?' asked Kizzy. 'Before it all goes wrong?'

Harper shook her head. 'I don't know, Kizzy. It's hard to concentrate when you don't know from one minute to the next what's going to— What's that?'

'Doorbell,' said Frazer. 'I'll go.'

'Be careful, darling – keep the chain on till you know who it is. It's almost dark out there.'

Frazer left the room and returned a moment later with Hazel Ratcliffe.

'Hazel!' Harper rose to greet her friend. 'What a lovely surprise, darling.'

They embraced and Hazel said, 'You sounded so down on the phone I thought I'd better dash over and stop you sticking your head in the disposomat.'

Harper laughed. 'It's not quite *that* bad, my dear. Not quite.'

'So.' Hazel sat down and crossed her legs. 'What's been happening, if anything? I want all the harrowing details.'

Harper and Kizzy brought Hazel up to date while Frazer brewed a pot of tea. The weather was too warm for the laser-blaze, so they sat round an empty hearth and talked as twilight gave way to night. The Ryes were no safer with Hazel there, but they *felt* more secure. She was that sort of person.

'What's been puzzling *me*,' said Harper after a while, 'is exactly what sort of weapon my apparatus might make. I mean – I'm assuming the M.o.D. has a weapon in mind.'

'Oh, that's easy,' said Hazel. 'I spent some time thinking about that, and I think I've got it.'

Harper looked at her. 'Go on.'

'Well.' Hazel took a sip of tea and set her cup and saucer on the small table in front of her. 'What your apparatus does is travel into the past, snatch some creature and transfer it instantly into the present – am I right?'

Harper nodded.

'And you can make this creature appear anywhere you like, yes? In this room, for example?'

'When things go right, yes.'

'OK then – imagine this scene. The leader of a nation at war with Britain has just out got of bed. It is seven a.m. He goes to the bathroom to shave. As he shaves, he is thinking about his day. Breakfast, then the drive to the office for a meeting with his generals. After that, papers to sign, then lunch, etcetera, etcetera, etcetera. You get the picture – an ordinary day in prospect. Suddenly – in the twinkling of an eye, as they say in fairytales – his bathroom vanishes. He's not looking into his shaving mirror any more. He's standing in a strange room a thousand miles away, dripping foam down his pyjamas and staring down the barrel of an automatic rifle. He's a prisoner in England, and it's the day after tomorrow.'

'My God!' Harper gazed at her friend.

'Well, yes – exactly,' said Hazel. 'He'd flip, wouldn't he? It'd blow his mind. And the folks back home would find themselves leaderless.'

'It's horrible,' breathed Kizzy. 'Surely nobody would actually *do* that to anybody?'

'They would, you know,' growled Frazer. 'Some people would do *anything* if it'll help 'em win.'

'I'm afraid Frazer's right,' murmured Harper. 'You've only to look at some of the weapons they *do* use – napalm, for example.' She shivered and looked across at her friend. 'What am I to *do*, Hazel? What on earth am I to do?'

FORTY-FOUR

'Just *look* at the time!' Hazel Ratcliffe started to rise. 'It's ten to eleven, these young people are still up and I have miles to go before I sleep.'

'It's these light evenings,' smiled Harper. 'They're deceptive.'

'Doesn't matter anyway,' said Frazer. 'I *never* have trouble getting up in the morning.'

'Huh!' grunted Kizzy. '*What* time was it when Bilbo woke you on Saturday?'

'That's different, you div – I was having a lie–in.

It's *you* who'll still be snoring at eight o'clock tomor—'

The crash of splintered glass was followed by a heavy thud as a mouldering brick landed on the carpet. The room's four occupants were staring at it when a man's voice shouted through the smashed window. 'We're here, Doctor Rye, just as I promised. Open the door and nobody'll get hurt.'

'It's Sefton,' hissed Frazer. 'I *told* you he was off his nut.'

'The gun!' cried Kizzy. 'Get the gun, Mum.'

Harper shook her head. 'The gun's useless, darling. I want you and Frazer to go upstairs at once. Don't switch on any lights, and stay away from the windows. I'm going to call the police.'

'*I'm* not off upstairs,' protested Frazer. 'There's doors to guard.'

'Well, *I'm* not if he's not,' said Kizzy. '*I'll* have the gun. It put Bilbo in hospital, even if it *is* useless.' She stretched up, lifted the weapon from its hooks and ran to the window.

'Kizzy!' Harper dashed after her as Hazel switched off the light.

'We've got a gun, Mr Sefton!' yelled Kizzy into the night. 'You come anywhere near this house and I'll blow your head off.'

Harper flung her arms round her daughter and dragged her to the floor as a second brick came hurtling out of the darkness and fell, its flight cut short by a heavy curtain.

'Harper, there's something wrong with the phone.' Hazel held the receiver in one hand and jiggled the button with the other. 'I think he's cut the line.'

'I'll try the extension.' Frazer dashed out of the room and up the stairs, but the bedroom extension was dead. 'You're right,' he called. 'The line's been cut.'

From the shadowy garden came a cracked laugh. 'It's been cut all right,' jeered Sefton. 'We're not amateurs, Doctor. You're up against a well-oiled machine here, so you might as well open the door and have done with it. We'll get in anyway, and your kids could be hurt in the process.'

Glass fragments tinkled as Harper got to her feet and peered out.

'You're insane, Sefton,' she cried. 'What d'you think you'd achieve if you *got* inside? You know nothing about my apparatus. You couldn't operate it.'

'No, but *you* could, and you will when we've got a knife at your kid's throat.'

'Never.'

'OK, Doctor – you've had your chance. We're coming in.'

A moment's silence, and then a whistle blew and the garden became filled with moving shadows and running footsteps.

Harper whirled. 'Upstairs!' she cried. 'Quickly. Get into one room and bar the door.'

'What about *you*, Mum?' Frazer had just come down.

Harper shook her head. 'Never mind about me – I must protect the apparatus. Just *go*, please.'

As she spoke there came a splintering crash, and the sound of running footsteps inside the house.

FORTY-FIVE

'Upstairs, the pair of you – go on.' Hazel flapped her hands at Frazer and Kizzy. Harper had disappeared towards her laboratory. There were noises from that direction – shouts and footfalls, and Hazel was anxious to follow her friend. She watched till the youngsters were halfway up the stairs, then hurried down the hallway.

As soon as she'd gone, Frazer said, 'Go on, Kizzy – barricade yourself in your room. I'm off to help.'

Kizzy opened her mouth to protest, but before she could utter a word her brother had vaulted the bannister and dashed off after Hazel.

Kizzy stood for a moment, listening. There seemed to be people everywhere. The house was full of their shouting, yet she couldn't see anybody. Martin Sefton and his friends had obviously broken into the house, but apart from that it was impossible to work out what was happening. Only one thing was certain – Kizzy was *not* about to barricade herself in her room. Brandishing the rusty gun as if she meant to use it, she tiptoed down the stairs and along the hallway, glancing back from time to time to make sure nobody was creeping up on her.

There was a man by the laboratory door. A big man with a bald head and clumpy boots, holding something which looked like a very long rounders bat. Kizzy dodged into a doorway and spied on him but he wasn't doing anything – just standing there.

The lab door was closed. When nobody was shouting or clomping, Kizzy could hear voices. One was Mum's, and there was a man, and another woman – probably Hazel. As Kizzy listened, the man started shouting. She couldn't make out what he was saying but he sounded furious. Mum and Hazel were obviously prisoners in the lab, and the man was probably trying to force Harper to operate the apparatus for him.

Where's Frazer? she wondered. Is he a prisoner too? If so, that just leaves me. What can I *do*? She thought for a moment, chewing her bottom lip. I suppose I could try sneaking out – phone the police. Trouble is, we've no neighbours and the nearest call-box is a couple of kilometres away.

She was still pondering on this when she heard heavy footfalls approaching. She was bound to be seen if she stayed where she was, so she eased open the door she'd been pressed up against, slipped through it, left it open a crack and stood with her eye to the crack. Two men clomped past. One of them said something to the man guarding the lab. Kizzy heard the door open and the same man said, 'We can't find the kid. We've had the place upside down.'

'Looked everywhere,' confirmed his companion.

'No you haven't!' shouted the man who'd been making all the noise. 'You haven't looked where she *is*, or you'd have found her.'

'If anything's happened to my — Ow!' Kizzy winced at the sound of the slap which cut off her mother's voice. It was as much as she could do to stop herself flinging open the door and charging along the hallway with the gun. The man's voice continued.

'Never mind. This dump's kilometres from any-where. She can't do anything. We'll be finished here soon anyway.' There was a moment's silence, then Kizzy jumped as a scream of pain rang out and the man's voice crooned, 'Isn't that right, Doctor Rye?'

Frazer! Kizzy gulped. They're hurting Frazer. Torturing him to make Mum do what they want. I've got to *do* something. Cautiously, she opened the door and peeped out. The bald man was standing by the lab door with the two who'd been searching for her. The door was open and they were looking in, grinning. As Kizzy eased herself into the hallway there was another scream and she heard Harper cry out, 'All right, all right – I'll do it.'

Hitler? Kizzy shuddered. She's going to snatch Hitler. He'll be in this house. In this time. It's sick. It's horrible. Frazer was right – Martin Sefton's crazy. Please let me get out. Don't let them look this way. Oh, please—

FORTY-SIX

She was lucky, or else her prayer was answered. None of the three men glanced in her direction as she sidled along the hallway and into the kitchen. Once there, she was out of sight. She crossed to the door, eased it open and looked out into the yard.

Nobody. OK then – let's get the bike. Quickly she crossed the yard, backed the bike out of the shed and wheeled it along the narrow path which ran down the side of the house. She stood for a moment in shadow, looking across the garden.

All seemed quiet. She'd left the gun in the shed, so speed was her only protection now. She mounted, stood on the pedals and set off diagonally across the lawn, praying that none of Sefton's lot would choose this moment to look through a window.

She'd made it through the gateway, turned right on to the track and was heading for the lane when there came a swishing and a crackling in the bushes and two figures burst out, blocking her way. Kizzy cried out and tried to swerve round them but the manoeuvre was too abrupt. The wheels skidded from under her and the bike crashed to the ground. She lay winded, looking up at the pale blobs of her captors' faces. It was then she saw that they were not Sefton's people, but Vulcan Pan's.

'Let me go,' she panted. 'Please. They've got my mum and brother. They're hurting them. I have to get to a phone.'

'We saw some guys,' said a woman's voice. 'Heard glass smashing. Who are they?'

'Sefton,' gasped Kizzy. 'He's crazy. He thinks Hitler should run the country. He's forcing Mum—'

'Oh my God!' cried the woman. 'I get the picture, kid.' She turned and yelled into the dark. 'Maureen – get over here, quick! Maureen's got a cellphone,' she explained. Hands were lifting Kizzy now – gentle hands that supported her and brushed the dirt from her clothes. 'Who were you calling, love?'

'The police,' said Kizzy. 'Please hurry – if I know Mum, she'll stall those guys as long as she can and that Sefton'll end up killing her.'

FORTY-SEVEN

Frazer lay face down on the bench with his collar in the goon's fist and his arm up his back. At a nod from Sefton, the goon cranked the boy's arm a little higher, causing him to cry out. Harper, at the console, spun round.

'Leave him alone, you great stupid bully – I'm working as fast as I can.'

Sefton smiled coldly. 'You don't look to be busting a gut from where I'm standing, Doctor.'

'It's a complicated procedure, you fool. How d'you

expect me to concentrate when that gorilla's torturing my son?'

The man shrugged. 'The torture, as you call it, will stop when our distinguised guest is standing in this room, and not before.'

Counting on Kizzy and stalling for all she was worth, Harper said, 'Do you speak German, Mr Sefton?'

'What?'

'I said, do you speak German? Your distinguished guest, as you call him, is likely to feel somewhat disorientated when he arrives. He'll need the situation explaining to him, and I'm not at all certain he spoke English.'

'*Speaks*,' rapped Sefton. 'Speaks, not spoke. And no, I don't speak German.'

Harper scoffed. 'And I don't need to ask whether *he* does.' She nodded towards the goon. 'I doubt if he speaks *human*, so how do you propose to greet your hero?'

'*I'll* worry about that,' snarled Sefton. 'You just get him here.'

'Don't, Mum,' gasped Frazer from the bench. 'Let 'em break my arm if they want to – it'll mend.'

'Don't you dare!' spat Hazel, glaring at Sefton from where she was sitting with her hands tied. 'You harm that boy and I'll see you put away for life.'

'Heroics, eh?' Sefton smiled thinly and nodded to the goon. 'Break his arm, Eric.'

'No!' Harper turned. 'I swear if you—'

There was a crash from somewhere in the house, followed at once by a cacophony of screams and yells. Sefton spun round and shouted to the trio in the doorway. 'See what that is. And don't let *anybody* approach this laboratory.'

The men started along the hallway, then stopped. 'What the heck—?'

'What *is* it?' bellowed Sefton. 'What's going on out there?' The screams and yells were deafening.

'It's – it's women,' stammered the sentry. 'A bunch of women, and a kid with a gun.'

'Damnation!' Sefton plunged a hand inside his jacket and pulled out a small automatic. 'Do I have to do *everything* myself around here?' He strode towards the door.

The hallway was jammed with screeching women in T–shirts. They had the three goons surrounded and were kicking and pummelling them as the men spun round and round, seeking space to swing their baseball bats. Between this mêlée and the laboratory door stood Kizzy, pointing her vintage gun at Sefton's chest.

'Drop that!' grated Sefton, levelling the automatic.

'You drop *that*,' shrilled Kizzy. What might have

happened next will never be known, because at that moment the wail of sirens rose above the din, followed by a screeching of brakes as many fast vehicles drew up outside the house. Blue flashes strobed through windows on to walls, floors and faces. Sefton stood a moment as though paralysed, then whirled with an oath and sprinted off along the hallway.

FORTY-EIGHT

The instant the goon realized Sefton wasn't coming back, he abandoned Frazer and fled the room.

Harper ran to her son. 'Darling – are you all right?' she said anxiously. He was sitting on the bench, massaging his arm.

'Bit sore, that's all. What the heck's happening?'

'Dunno exactly. Listen.' She spoke rapidly, watching the door. 'I've come to a decision, and I need a few minutes. I want you to untie Hazel and get her out of here so I can lock myself in. The police have arrived, and I suspect the M.o.D aren't far behind. I need you to block up that hallway for as long as you can. Will you do it?'

Frazer slid off the bench. 'You – you're not going to *hurt* yourself or anything, are you, Mum?'

'No, of course not, silly. Hurry now.'

Hazel's wrists were bound with parcel tape. Frazer ripped it away, pulled the woman to her feet and the two of them left the laboratory. Harper slammed the door behind them. They heard the key turn in the lock. To their left the three goons, now disarmed, staggered about the hallway, trying desperately to dislodge the fans of Vulcan Pan who clung to their limbs and clothing as though to their hero himself, while Kizzy danced round the fringe of the mêlée, cracking the occasional shin with the butt of her gun. As Frazer and Hazel moved to join in, a squad of armed policemen burst through the kitchen doorway. Their leader, an inspector, raised his revolver, fired a shot into the ceiling and yelled, 'M.o.D. police – stand where you are!'

The mêlée became a tableau as the participants turned to find themselves staring down the barrels of half a dozen automatic rifles. Everybody froze except Kizzy, who bent down very slowly, laid her gun on the floor and straightened up, watching the policemen the whole time.

The inspector glanced from face to startled face. 'Which one of you is Doctor Rye?' Frazer looked sidelong at Hazel and pulled a face. Harper had had less than a minute so far.

Hazel nodded imperceptibly and lifted her hand. 'I am.'

The man rapped an order to his squad and strode over. 'Take me to your laboratory, please, Doctor.'

'Certainly,' murmured Hazel. 'This way, Officer.' She turned and led the man past the laboratory door.

Frazer watched till the two of them turned left into a disused former dining-room, then turned and grinned at his sister. 'Nice one, Sis.'

The policemen had separated the goons from the girls and were leading both groups from the house. As Frazer spoke, a constable bent to retrieve the ancient gun. He straightened up, looked at the two youngsters and said, 'Come on – you two as well.'

'But we *live* here,' protested Kizzy. 'Doctor Rye's our mother.'

The man nodded. 'Stay out of the way then, and you'll be all right.'

He was moving away when the inspector reappeared, leading Hazel Ratcliffe by the arm.

'Fitzwilliam.'

'Sir?'

The officer nodded towards the laboratory door. 'Open that.'

The constable tried the door. 'It's locked, sir.'

'Then smash it in, man.'

'Yessir.' He lifted Kizzy's gun and began battering at the wood around the lock. Frazer looked at his watch. Four minutes, if that. He hoped it had been long enough.

At the seventh blow the timber gave and the door flew open. Acrid smoke spilled into the hallway.

'Mum!'

Frazer rushed forward but the constable grabbed his arm.

'Wait here. *And* you,' he added, as Kizzy started to move.

'Take 'em outside,' rapped the inspector. 'I'll talk to them later.'

The constable ushered the trio away. The inspector pulled out a handkerchief, held it over his nose and mouth and walked into the laboratory. He didn't know exactly what he'd expected to see, but a bare floor and a smashed console out of which issued smoke and blue sparks certainly wasn't it. His smarting eyes darted about the room and came to rest on the woman.

'Where's the time machine?'

'*Time* machine?' Harper's dirt-streaked face creased into a smile which left a sadness in her eyes. 'What d'you think you're on, Inspector – *Doctor Who*?'

FORTY-NINE

'What did you *do*, Mum?' asked Kizzy, as Hazel's
Euro bore them towards Ipswich. The inspector had
finished with the Ryes for the moment but his men
were still ransacking the house, so Hazel was taking
them to stay with her for a few days.

Harper sighed. 'I destroyed it, darling. There was
no alternative.'

'In four minutes?' gasped Frazer. 'You smashed
it up in four minutes? What about the bits, Mum
– won't they be able to reconstruct it from the
bits?'

Harper laughed. 'There are no bits, darling. I didn't destroy it in the lab. I'm not *that* daft. I piled all my papers into it and sent the whole caboodle into the past – two thousand years into the past – and to make absolutely sure, I dumped it in the mouth of an active volcano.' She smiled. 'So – those boys back there are searching in vain. There's nothing left but some shorted-out circuitry which might have been used for anything.'

Hazel looked sidelong at her friend. 'You sound remarkably cheerful,' she said, 'for someone who's just scuppered her chance of fame and fortune. Aren't you sad at all?'

Harper nodded. 'Oh yes, dear. I regret the destruction of Rye's Apparatus, but my regret is outweighed by relief – relief that I was able to prevent my invention's use as a weapon. It can never harm anybody now, you see.'

'Mum?' Kizzy's voice sounded odd.

Harper looked at her. 'What is it, darling?'

'Which year did the apparatus end up in?'

Harper shrugged. 'I don't know, dear – not exactly. There wasn't time for pinpoint accuracy, except for dropping the thing into the volcano, of course. Why d'you ask?'

'But you think it was two thousand years ago?'

'Give or take a couple of centuries, yes.'

'Which volcano?'

Harper smiled. 'Guess.'

'I don't want to.'

'Which volcano would *you* have chosen?' pressed Harper. 'Which name comes into your mind whenever you hear the *word* volcano?'

'Vesuvius,' murmured Kizzy.

'Well, there you are then,' she chuckled. 'Vesuvius it was.'

'It's not funny, Mum.'

'Isn't it?' Harper gazed at her daughter. 'You're a strange one, Kizzy – you really are. You behave heroically in the face of all that hassle, and then when it's over you go all solemn on us. What is it?'

Kizzy shook her head. 'It doesn't matter.'

'Yes it *does*,' insisted Harper. 'Tell us.'

Kizzy sighed. 'You say Rye's Apparatus never hurt anybody and never will, right?'

Harper nodded.

'Well – in seventy-nine AD Mount Vesuvius erupted, smothering the towns of Pompeii and Herculaneum and the settlement at Stabia. Thousands died.' Kizzy looked at her mother. 'Seventy-nine AD is two thousands years ago, give or take a couple of centuries. What *made* it erupt, Mum? Could it have erupted because a machine from the future dropped into it?'

'I – I don't believe—' Harper's voice tailed off. Nobody else had anything to say. The Euro sped through the dark.

THE END

ABOUT THE AUTHOR

Robert Swindells left school at fifteen and worked as a copyholder on a local newspaper. At seventeen he joined the RAF for three years, two of which he served in Germany. He then worked as a clerk, an engineer and a printer before training and working as a teacher. He is now a full-time writer and lives on the Yorkshire moors.

He has written many books for young readers, including *Inside The Worm*, *Room 13*, *Hydra* and *Nightmare Stairs,* all of which are also available in Corgi Yearling paperback. *Room 13* won the 1990 Children's Book Award and *Abomination* won the Stockport Children's Book Award and was shortlisted for the Whitbread Award. His books for older readers include *Stone Cold*, which won the 1994 Carnegie Medal.

HYDRA
Robert Swindells

The floater moved out into the barn. Eyeless, it felt the faint pull of starlight and followed, passing through the great open doorway and drifting away in the dark . . .

Friends Ben and Midge are determined to investigate when mysterious corn circles begin to appear in the fields around Cansfield Farm. But when they sneak out at night to explore, they discover that the corn circles are not the only mystery at the farm; a dilapidated barn conceals a terrifying secret. As Midge and Ben uncover the true horror that is being spawned there, they know that they must tell someone, warn them of the danger. But who will believe their incredible story?

'Spine-chilling suspense' *Junior Education*

'Compelling' *The School Librarian*

A FEDERATION OF CHILDREN'S BOOK
GROUPS PICK OF THE YEAR

0 440 86313 9

ABOMINATION
Robert Swindells

Martha is twelve, and very different from other
kids. No TV. No computer. No cool clothes.
Especially, no *friends*.

It's all because of her parents. Strict members of a
religious group, their rules dominate Martha's life.
But one rule is the most important of all: Martha
must never *ever* invite anyone home. If she does,
their terrible secret – Abomination – could be
revealed . . .

A chilling and thought-provoking tale for older
readers from the bestselling author of the award-
winning *Room 13*, *Nightmare Stairs* and many other
titles.

'A taut and thrilling novel from a master of the
unpredictable'
Daily Telegraph

0 440 86362 7

CORGI YEARLING BOOKS

All Transworld titles are available by post from:

**Book Service By Post, P.O. Box 29,
Douglas, Isle of Man IM99 1BQ**

Credit cards accepted.
Please telephone 01624 675137, fax 01624 670923,
or Internet http://www.bookpost.co.uk or e-mail:
bookshop@enterprise.net for details.

Free postage and packing in the UK.
Overseas customers allow £1 per book (paperbacks) and £3 per book
(hardbacks).